JONAS McFEE, A.T.P.

JONAS McFEE, A.T.P.

by Sarah Sargent

Bradbury Press
New York

Bradbury Press
An Affiliate of Macmillan, Inc.
866 Third Avenue, New York, NY 10022
Collier Macmillan Canada, Inc.
First Edition
Printed and bound in the United States of America
10 9 8 7 6 5 4 3 2 1

The text of this book is set in 12 point Caledonia.

Book design by Julie Quan
LIBRARY OF CONGRESS CATALOGING-IN-PUBLICATION DATA
Sargent, Sarah.
Jonas McFee, A.T.P.
Summary: Fifth-grader Jonas McFee faces the
temptation of becoming the Awful Terrible Powerful
One when he accidentally acquires a blue crystal
from outer space, giving him the power to get China
on his television and make his car fly.
[1. Science fiction] I. Title.
PZ7.S2479Jo 1989 [Fic] 88-19245
ISBN 0-02-778041-4

For Edgar

JONAS McFEE, A.T.P.

1

JONAS McFEE was the new kid. He was butting into the class in February after everybody was used to everybody and all the best friends were paired off. Making it worse, he was small and wore glasses. February was basketball season. Every fifth-grade kid in America was bopping that ball up to the hoop at recess.

"What'd you say your name was?"

Jonas steeled himself. In class he'd caught on that Sean Murdock was the kid everybody looked to. He was tall and skinny and always moving a little. He bounced and swayed in his desk across from Jonas while they worked math problems. Now, at recess, Jonas knew Sean had thought of some way to make a joke about Jonas's name. Jonas pushed his glasses up on his nose, feeling trapped. He never could think of what to say at times like this.

"Jonas McFee." He'd finally given up and just blurted out his name, though he knew he was asking for it. "My name is Jonas McFee." He hated himself.

"What's that? *Bone Ass?* Bone Ass McFueeh?" Sean said *McFee* like a sneeze, sucking in his lip for the *Mc* and blowing out on the *Fee.* "Must make it hard, sitting on something like that. You bring a pillow or what?"

He danced up toward Jonas, dribbling the ball, looking over his shoulder at the other kids in a circle around him. They all laughed, though it was one of the dumbest jokes Jonas had ever heard. Jonas hated Sean, he hated the school, he hated his mom for dragging him off in the middle of the year this way.

Quickly he looked over the playground. He needed to find a way to be doing something so no teacher would feel sorry for him and force kids to "include" him. Jogging would be okay. He could run along the chain-link fence. Jonas liked to run. He was good at it. Kids here would find that out. He would have friends once he figured out how to get past Sean Murdock.

Maybe he could do something with *his* name. Jonas tried to think while he jogged, listening to the thud, thud, thud of his sneakers. "Sean . . . dawn . . . fawn . . ." Nothing halfway decent was coming. He was still too mad to think straight.

The wind made his eyes water. The shouts of

the kids playing basketball and the chants of a group jumping rope faded as he jogged the length of the block. He was into the section where first and second graders climbed on rubber tires. Two of them came rolling toward the fence like fat puppies in the snowsuits their moms made them wear, fanning the air with mittened hands, not really hitting each other. Jonas stopped, a little winded anyway, to let them move out of his way. He leaned his cheek against the thick wire of the fence.

His old school had had grass in the playground. This one had black tar and a steel fence. Crumpled papers and smashed pop cans had blown into the corners. He felt like a piece of trash himself, piling all his stuff in their brown beater of a car that used to be a taxi, going wherever his mom wanted.

While he was standing feeling sorry for himself, a bus came along and hissed open its back door. A girl jumped off.

She was small, not much taller than he was, but she was older. Thirteen at least. Her face was pale; her hair was blue-black. As soon as her feet hit the sidewalk, she whirled around, staring in all directions. Her eyes met Jonas's. He had never seen anyone so scared. Her skin looked stretched, her eyes enormous.

"Here!" She held something in her fingers through a space in the wire mesh. "Take this. Keep it. I'll be back." Jonas didn't think to say no. He held out his hand, and she dropped a small blue ball into it. He opened his mouth to tell her he couldn't keep it, but she was gone. As soon as his fingers closed around the ball, she left, running fast as the wind down the street.

"Hey! I can't . . ." The words died in Jonas's throat.

A skinny man with a long horseface was thudding down the sidewalk toward Jonas. He was wearing a bottle green coat two sizes too big that billowed behind him. He didn't notice Jonas, who pulled back a step or two from the fence as the man came even with him.

His lip was curled back in a snarl, and his eyes gleamed in slits, a yellow brown, the same as the girl's. He must have jumped off the bus as soon as it stopped, and run back to catch the girl. Jonas folded his hand around the ball and tried to swallow past the lump of fear in his throat. Suppose the man glanced into the playground and saw the look on his face? But he whizzed on past, his beaklike nose quivering in the cold wind, like a hound's.

"Here," said Jonas, "were you looking for this?" And then hated himself for being chicken.

But he spoke to the empty air. The man was long gone. Behind him, the bell rang, surprising him. Jonas stuffed the ball into his jacket pocket and headed for the building, glad to go inside.

*J*ONAS'S BEDROOM wasn't set up yet. His bed was against the wall, and the bureau was beside it, but he hadn't had time to tape up his posters or unpack his games and clothes. The electronic robot his granddad had given him for Christmas was standing in the corner by the closet, its remote control on his bed.

He'd run it so much it was already out of batteries. Jonas loved the way the little guy marched along, turning to the left and right when he pushed the control stick. The robot had a voice program, too, for doing math problems and answering geography questions. Jonas's granddad wanted to be sure he was learning school kinds of things.

Where should he put the blue ball? Even alone in his room, Jonas felt nervous with it out in the open. It was the size of a big marble, a cloudy blue. It felt like glass. If he'd seen it on the sidewalk, Jonas wouldn't have looked at it twice.

"Out of sight, out of mind." That was a saying of his mom's when she shoved the phone bill into the sock drawer, months when they were short. Jonas creaked open the closet door and rolled the little ball across the floor toward the darkest corner. Jonas stared. In the dark the ball glowed. A pale blue light shone for two or three feet around it. Not only that, but the circle of light kept changing. The ball was still, but its light went bright and dim, and cast odd floating shadows on his closet walls. He slammed the door shut behind him and leaned against it, the knob in his back.

He heard a key in the apartment door. His mom was home from work. Jonas's mouth was dry. He'd planned to have the ball put away and to be in the living room acting normal by the time his mom came home. The first few weeks when she started a new job, Jonas had learned to be careful around his mom.

She didn't have an easy life. Sometimes when he saw the moms on TV, worrying about their kitchen floors being shiny, Jonas had to laugh. His mom didn't have time to care if she could see her face in their floor. She was trying to save up to pay the rent and all the other bills. She wanted to take classes and learn to do more.

His granddad talked to him about her, about how hard it was for her, so he would understand if she was cross sometimes. Jonas tried, but he had a hard time being nice. On TV, kids had so much money. They all had computers and laser guns.

"Jones? You home?" He heard the rustle of grocery bags being piled on the table. He relaxed. That was what she called him when she was feeling good. He went to help her unpack the soup and hot dogs.

After they had everything put away, his mom started to heat some spaghetti and went to soak in the tub until it was ready. Jonas didn't really want to go back to his room, but he couldn't stop thinking about the flashing lights in his closet. The ball pulled him back like a magnet.

He crept into the dark room and cracked open the closet door. The ball must be resting. There was just a faint light around it, a quiet glow. He shut the door and lay on his bed to think. The control stick for his robot was under him. Moving it out of the way, Jonas accidentally pushed it to the ON position. No matter, since it wasn't working anyway. He lay back and stared up at the ceiling, going through what had happened at recess. The girl had looked so afraid. He tried not to think about the man.

An odd humming noise made him sit up. The robot was marching stiff-legged across the room toward him, all its colored bulbs glowing bright. Jonas's eyes widened. He *knew* those batteries were dead. Could they have come back after sitting for a while? Gotten recharged from resting? He frowned. If so, he'd never heard of it.

The robot kept coming. Jonas took the stick and pushed it left to make the robot turn. Instead, the robot stopped, swaying back and forth on its shiny silver boots. Its hinged mouth opened, even though Jonas had not put a voice disk into the slot on its back.

"Ahhvul Toval Pohpar," it said in a deep voice. At least, as near as Jonas could make out, that's what it said. It was *supposed* to say things like "The capital of Nebraska is Lincoln," or "Twenty times four is eighty." That was all it had ever said before. And its real voice was squeaky. This voice sounded like the wind blowing under the door in a storm. "Ahhvul Toval Pohpar," it said again.

"Who's that, Jonesie?" his mom called from the bathroom.

Hand trembling, Jonas pushed the stick to OFF. "Ahh . . ." the thing said, and stopped. Jonas was shaking. He climbed off the bed and went to the door.

"It was just my robot," he said. "The batteries are shot."

"Yuck," his mom said, coming out of the bath-room in her robe, running her fingers through her wet hair. "Creepy. Sounded like an old mon-ster movie. The part where the mummy was just about to *grab* you." She snatched at Jonas's ear. He ducked and tried to laugh.

3

THAT NIGHT before he went to bed Jonas shut the robot in the closet with the ball. He was afraid of both of them. The ball must be an energy source, making the batteries work again. But whose voice was coming out of the robot? What was the blue ball making it say?

"Ahhvul Toval Pohpar . . ." The only language Jonas had ever heard besides English was German. The robot wasn't speaking that, either.

He could open the window and throw the ball out. Let it bounce down the street. The robot would go back to normal without the ball. But he didn't want to touch either of them. Jonas just wanted to go to sleep and pretend none of it had ever happened. He crunched under the covers, tight as a ball himself, and pictured his old room before this one. He told himself he was back home, just down the block from his granddad. That way, he finally went to sleep.

The next morning, the sun was shining. Jonas

sat up and looked away from the closet door. He hadn't hung up his clothes yet, so he didn't need to open it. He ate a bowl of cereal after his mom left and then locked up and headed for school. From a block away, he could see the girl who had given him the ball standing beside the fence, looking up and down the sidewalk at the kids coming toward her. She spotted him and stepped forward.

"I come for the ball. I thank you for it." His grandmother had talked like that. She had come from the old country.

"It's at home. In my closet. I didn't know you would be here."

Her light brown eyes grew round. "I must have ball. You must give me back the ball." She grabbed Jonas's sleeve. For a second, he was scared. But seeing how desperate she looked, he felt sorry for her.

"Yes." Jonas pulled his arm free. "I don't want your ball. You can have it. Meet me after school. Come home with me, and I will give it to you. Okay?"

"After school?" She pointed to a watch on her wrist.

"Two forty-five," Jonas said. "Quarter to three. I get out then."

"We will meet then? You will show me to your home? Give me the ball?"

"Yes. Yes. I want to get rid of it. Meet me here. I'll see you then." Jonas ducked away from her. Kids had looked at him funny while he stood talking to her. He didn't want people thinking he had a weird sister or anything like that. He ran inside the building, glad to escape.

When he came out of school, she was in the same spot beside the fence. He was so glad that it was all going to be over that he almost ran toward her. But she was not alone. The man in the green coat had his hand on her shoulder in a way that could have looked friendly, but Jonas could see that he was holding her.

Jonas didn't know what to do. When the girl spotted him, he saw fear in her eyes. She looked away. She was going to pretend not to know him. Jonas walked toward them, acting as if he were busy sorting through the lunch tickets in his wallet. The girl looked so small with that man clutching her. Jonas could hardly swallow, walking toward them.

"Which is the one? You show me the one. I am not a fool. Someone is helping you. You will both die. I am Pohpar. . . ." His voice lowered to a hiss. Jonas, white as a sheet, hurried past. "You will show me the one." The man's voice floated behind him, raised again and icy cold. Jonas made himself walk for a whole block. Then he ran the rest of the way as fast as he could. He saw the girl's white still face as he clumped up the stairs to his door. What would the man do to her? The proud way she stood there, looking straight ahead, made him shiver.

4

AFTER SCHOOL, Jonas usually had a peanut butter sandwich and a glass of milk. He forced himself to fix the sandwich as usual, but the first bite just sat in his throat. He was too scared to swallow. He took a gulp of milk to wash the lump of sandwich down, then dropped the rest of it into the garbage and poured his milk down the sink.

Maybe he could watch a little TV until his mother came home, to take his mind off the man. He went into the living room and snapped the set on. Snow. He changed the channel. More snow, and static on the sound track.

"Adrian knew that Catherine was going to have the baby. But when Emily learns that Patrick told Susan . . ."

Some dumb soap opera was the only thing that would come in. They hadn't hooked up an antenna yet. He had almost two hours in the apartment by himself. What could he do besides sit and shake, thinking about the man at the playground?

Jonas thought of something. At first, he wasn't sure his idea was really good—it might be crazy. Besides, it meant touching the ball, going and getting it out of the closet. He couldn't do that. Jonas fingered the little hole in the arm of the sofa, pushing his finger in and out. He chewed his lower lip and pulled on his earlobe, hesitating.

He'd brought it home, hadn't he? And it hadn't hurt him. Anyway, Jonas didn't really think the girl would have given it to him if it were dangerous that way. She didn't look like that sort of person.

What he was thinking was, *If the blue ball makes the robot work, what will it do for the TV?* He was there. The ball was there. Not much he could do about that. If he was going to have to sit, thinking about the ball, he might as well try to *use* it, Jonas told himself. The girl gave him the ball to keep for her; he ought to find out about it.

Jonas marched into his room and opened the closet door, humming a little under his breath the way his granddad did when he was doing something a little tricky like fixing the toaster. Was he imagining it, or was the ball warm in the palm of his hand? Did he feel it pulsing like something electrical?

Jonas carried the ball loosely, trying to hold it away from his skin. He dropped it beside the TV set and shoved it partway under to stop its rolling. He used one finger, his heart pounding. Then he backed away, toward the sofa. He'd rest a minute before he tried the channels again.

But he'd left the set on. All of a sudden a picture was coming in clear as day. It was a cowboy movie, and he could see every leaf on the trees, the sweat on the horse's rump. Their TV had never had a clear picture. Not in its whole miserable life. Jonas's mom had spent hours turning knobs and adjusting the brightness and smacking the side of the cabinet, but no place that they had ever lived had had good reception. Now look! Jonas couldn't believe it. He jumped up and clicked the channel changer. Every spot had something on, and every single channel was as clear as the first.

Jonas was so excited that he leaned against the set and bumped the ball back a few inches. The picture changed. He was afraid he'd ruined it. Maybe it was going to be hard to figure out just where to place the ball along the set. But, no. All that had happened was that the channel had changed.

An ad was coming on, and it was for a shopping mall in Washington, D.C. Jonas flipped the dial. It was the half-hour break—stations were identifying themselves. He saw that several others were in Washington. Jonas moved the ball back a few more inches. Again, the channels shifted to a different city. The networks were the same, of course, and there were a lot of preachers on, but it was fantastic, the number of programs he could get.

He found that just a slight shift, a jiggle in the ball's position, gave him a whole new set of channels. Just by putting it on one side of the TV he tuned in to so many different cities he lost count. New York, Houston, places he'd never heard of—Santa Fe and Orlando and Seattle. All the TV in the United States was here, on his TV set. It was unbelievable.

Jonas picked up the ball and shoved it up against the set on the other side. The picture was still clear, but the sound was funny. The people were speaking another language. Gently he edged the ball along. The languages changed, but he still couldn't understand them. Clearly, the set was bringing in all the TV in the *world*. Jonas staggered back and sat down. No wonder that guy wanted this ball. Who wouldn't? It was fantastic. And it would have to be worth a fortune.

5

JONAS SPENT an hour experimenting, making himself dizzy watching TV from everywhere. He was dying to have somebody to watch with him. But he didn't have a friend at school yet. And he felt deep down that he should not tell anyone about the ball, however much he wanted to. Not until he understood a little more himself. He wouldn't even tell his mom, though he would love to show her how well it made the TV work.

She might make him give it back. Maybe she'd throw it out the window, the way Jonas had thought of doing himself, if he told her about the man in the green coat. Or call in the police or other people, the way grown-ups usually did.

He could go his whole life and not have a chance like this, Jonas thought. Something truly amazing to figure out. When he had run in from school, he had hated the ball and almost hated the girl for leaving it. Now he was wondering if having it might not turn out to be the most wonderful thing that could have happened to him. What else might it do? Before he gave it back—*if* he gave it back, he was on the edge of thinking— he needed to know more about its powers. "Finders, keepers," they used to say at his old school.

He went over to the set and held the ball in his fingers, bolder now. It wasn't going to hurt him. He moved it around to the front of the set, held it between his thumb and one finger, directly in front of the screen. What sort of picture would that make?

"Ahhvul Toval Pohpar . . ." The voice came, deep and strong, as it had from the little robot. Jonas almost dropped the ball. He forced himself to stand still.

"Can't you speak English?" He stared at the screen, which was full of boiling greenish clouds, like the view from an airplane window in a world with a sky that was another color than blue. It was a dumb question, which Jonas just blurted out because he was so sick of those words and of the way he felt weak at the sound of them.

"Yes."

He stared at the screen and tried to swallow. His throat was dry. "You can?" he said, dazed.

"I can." It sounded a little like the girl, like someone speaking a language that wasn't really natural.

"I am Jonas McFee," he said. "Are you named Ahhvul Toval Pohpar?"

"No," the voice answered.

"What do those words mean?" Jonas asked. "Can you tell me that? *Ahhvul Toval Pohpar?*" His own voice trembled.

"*Ahhvul*—'awful,' *Toval*—'terrible,' *Pohpar*—'powerful one,'" the voice replied. It sure didn't waste words on extras. Jonas shuddered, picturing the mean-faced man in the flowing green coat. He must be the awful terrible powerful one. He looked it. Jonas wondered if he had any other name.

"Who is the Ahhvul Toval Pohpar?" he asked the screen.

"Jonas McFee," the voice answered simply.

Jonas dropped the ball. It rolled across the floor and went under the couch. The bulging green clouds faded from the screen, and a regular TV voice came on.

"You mean you thought this was my natural color?"

A lady was talking about dyeing her hair. Jonas listened to her tell about how she was having a "whole family" to dinner while he crawled under the sofa to retrieve the ball. Was the voice making fun of him? But it sounded like a robot voice. Computers didn't know how to joke around.

He reached the ball with the tips of his fingers

and brushed it toward him. He dusted himself off and grasped the ball between his fingers again. The lady was just fluffing her hair one last time when he held the ball up and replaced her with the green clouds.

"Jonas McFee is the Ahhvul Toval Pohpar?" he asked, keeping his voice surprisingly steady.

"Affirmative."

Jonas made a face. The thing wouldn't go on to tell you what you wanted to know. You had to think just what to ask it. He knew that was the way computers worked. He thought for a minute.

"Why is Jonas McFee the Ahhvul Toval Pohpar?" he finally asked.

"Because he holds the blue ball." The answer came back clear and simple. "The one who holds the blue ball is the Ahhvul Toval Pohpar."

Jonas stood still for a minute, letting the information sink in. He reached over and switched off the TV set. For now, that was all he wanted to know. He felt different. He walked into the bathroom, where there was a mirror. He thought his face looked more serious, older.

He swelled out his nostrils, the way he'd seen tough guys do on TV, just before they pulled the trigger. He turned his head to the side to try and see himself in profile, jutting his chin out. "Jonas McFee is the Awful Terrible Powerful One," he

whispered, making his voice deep, looking sidewise at himself in the mirror. Jonas McFee,
A.T.P. He could have cards printed up. The door
in the living room opened.

"Jonesie?" His mom was home. Jonas dropped
the ball into his pocket.

"Yeah, Mom. I'm here." He went in to meet
her.

"*I'M BUSHED*," his mom said, collapsing into
the armchair with her legs straight out like sticks.
"What do you say we live it up and go out to
eat?"

Normally this question delighted Jonas. He
loved getting a burger and fries or splitting a
pizza for dinner. Just being able to walk in and
pick what he wanted always made him feel
important. But that was before this afternoon.
Should the Awful Terrible Powerful One walk
into McDonald's and order a chocolate shake and
a cheeseburger with fries?

Suppose they ran into that man? Jonas was
sure his face would give him away. The man
would know he had the ball. Before, Jonas had
been dying to get rid of the ball. He had wanted
to leave it in the darkest corner of the closet and
pretend it didn't exist. Now he didn't want to
leave it behind for a minute. He was determined

to keep the ball in his pocket, but he was afraid to go out of the house with it.

"You okay?" His mom sat up straight and frowned.

"Sure. Yeah. I'm good. I was just thinking. How come we never order in? We could just call, and one of those pizza places would deliver. Then we could eat here."

"Here?" His mom looked around.

Jonas followed her glance. There was a streak down one wall where the roof must have leaked. The landlord was supposed to have painted it before they moved in, but he hadn't. The carpet was an ugly gold color, and it had a spot just by the door. The place wasn't exactly pretty, Jonas would have to say. It was what they could afford and it was all right, but it wasn't anywhere you'd just hate to leave.

"Well, we might get a phone call or something," Jonas said uneasily. "Suppose Granddad tries to call?"

"Why would he?" His mom looked blank. "We talked to him just after we got here. Jonas, do you know something I don't?" She came over and felt his forehead. "No fever. What's up?"

Jonas gave up. "You're always talking about spending money—that's all," he muttered. "I was just trying to be responsible." She was always telling him that.

She rumpled his hair. "You're a good kid, Jonesie," she said, relief in her voice. "But don't worry. We can afford to eat out once in a while. Put on your jacket and let's go. You can choose."

In the car, he kept his hand in his pocket, his fingers loosely around the ball. Jonas was thinking. Their old beater of a car embarrassed him, backfiring and releasing clouds of smelly smoke. Suppose the ball could do something for the car the way it did for the TV? He shifted it in his hand until it was between his thumb and forefinger. Somehow he had learned that that was the power position. That was the way he had held it to make the voice come from the TV.

Sure enough, under his thumb he felt a slight jolt, as if he had turned the power on. Inside his pocket, so his mom wouldn't see, he aimed the ball toward the engine, pointing it more or less straight ahead and holding it steady. *Make it run smooth*, he thought, concentrating so hard he squinted his eyes shut. *Fix this miserable engine.*

His mom turned the key and stepped on the gas. Usually it coughed once or twice and cut off. Usually she had to turn the key on and off and pump the gas to get the monster to move. This time, the engine purred. It sounded brand-new.

"Hey," his mom said, "I told you this car wasn't so bad, Jonesie. Just needs to get warmed up a little." She pulled away from the curb and headed down the street. Jonas stretched to see out the back window. There was no cloud of smoke trailing behind them. He settled back into the seat with a little smile.

Jonas was leaning back imagining that he was a rock star in a limo, surrounded by a ton of cream-colored Cadillac buffed to a satin sheen. It was easy to make it seem real, the way this baby was humming along.

Let's just float on down the street, he said to himself. *Like riding on air.*

"Whaaah!" His mom's squawk brought him back to reality.. She was clutching the wheel, her knuckles white. "It's off the ground!" she shrieked. "Jonas, I swear, this thing is flying."

Opening his eyes, Jonas felt his stomach floating out from under him the way it did when he got onto an elevator. "Down," he said, as if he were yelling at a bad dog. Thud. The tires sank back to the street.

"That didn't happen," his mom said, breathing hard. "That can't *possibly* have happened." Fortunately, she had been too upset herself to notice anything Jonas had said. She drove along for a half block in silence, loosening her grip on the wheel. "I guess it must have been the suspension, Jonesie," she said after a while. "It is a little loose or whatever. Probably the springs stretched a little too much, gave the illusion of flying."

"That makes sense," Jonas said, shifting the ball out of the power position. The car went back to its rattles and gasps. He was almost glad to hear them.

7

JONAS McFEE, A.T.P. He could get China on his TV, and he could make his car fly. He would just have to learn to know his own strength, that was all. He'd never hold the ball in the power position and daydream, that was for sure. Jonas lay awake for an hour after he went to bed and pictured the scene at recess tomorrow. He wanted every detail perfect. No loose ends like in the car. Finally he turned over to sleep, satisfied.

"Enjoy your last night, Sean Murdock," he muttered, chuckling into his pillow. "Your last night as boss of the fifth grade."

Jonas had to leave early the next morning because he was going to school a different way. He walked three blocks extra and came to the building from the opposite direction. He knew that the girl—if she was still alive—would watch for him on the other side. So would the man in the green coat. He kept fingering the round lump in his jeans pocket, checking every second to be sure it was there.

The human brain is a kind of computer. It works by electrical impulses. So the ball *ought* to work on people, too. Jonas told himself his thinking was airtight, but he was nervous. If the plan didn't work, he'd end up looking like an even worse idiot than he had when Sean went after his name in the first place.

"Nothing risked, nothing gained." His granddad said that all the time.

"Nothing risked, nothing lost, either," Jonas muttered. Last night, the plan had had him rolling from side to side, chuckling in bed. Now it seemed a lot less foolproof. Jonas walked in the side door and headed for the fifth grade room.

At recess Sean Murdock and his crowd assembled as usual in front of the basketball hoop. They ignored Jonas. His hands were cold and sweaty, but he walked up to Sean.

"What's your name, kid?" His voice dipped a little. He had the ball firmly between his first finger and thumb. Both hands were in his pockets. He felt like the private eye in a TV crime show.

"You know my name." Sean sounded a little surprised, but mostly just bored. He didn't think Jonas was worth spending time on twice. Once had put him in his place.

"Gee, I forget, though," Jonas said slowly.

"*Yawn* I think you said. *Yawn Burdock*." Burdocks were prickly nettles Jonas helped his granddad pull off his dog's coat. They did remind him of Sean. "Nothing in this world but pure nuisances," his granddad always said about them.

Sean snorted and shook his head. "Forget it, kid. *Yawn* . . . that's the dumbest . . ." He stopped, his mouth stretched in a huge yawn. "What the . . .?" Immediately, another yawn. You could fit an orange inside that gaping trap of his—a grapefruit, Jonas told himself, delighted. The others stared wide-eyed.

"What's going on?" Randy Messerich asked him. "How are you doing that?"

"Do you have some sort of powder or something?" Juan Fernandez took a step backward. "I've heard about itching powder and something that makes people sneeze."

Jonas shook his head. "It's a kind of hypnotic power," he said, trying not to brag. "I only use it once in a while. I have to be careful." He looked at Sean, who was still yawning and still trying to sputter out words between times.

"Cut it . . ."—yawn—". . . stop . . ."—yawn. Jonas released the ball, pushing it down in his pocket. Sean stopped yawning. He rubbed his jaw and eyed Jonas nervously. Jonas almost laughed out loud. But he wanted to keep a cool image.

"You okay?" He sounded worried. "I didn't want to hurt you. Like I said, I try to be careful."

Sean glared at him. "You didn't hurt me. I'm fine." He started to turn away. He did dribble the ball a couple of times. Jonas saw Sean hoped he could get the game going as if nothing had happened. But, like the others, he was dying to know how Jonas made him yawn. "Hypnotic powers, did you say? What else can you do?"

Jonas saw it was killing him to ask. "Oh, not much," Jonas said modestly. He looked at each kid in the circle that had formed around him. "Unless you think things like making watches run weird and that sort of stuff is a big deal."

"Does it hurt the watch?" Juan was wearing a calendar digital with a shiny stainless-steel band. Jonas shook his head.

"Let's see, Juan. What is your favorite day? Tomorrow's Saturday, right? Let's just speed that baby on up to Saturday noon." Jonas reached deep in his pocket and caught the ball. He aimed toward Juan's wrist and closed his eyes, concentrating.

"That's amazing!" All the kids were clustered around Juan's wrist. He stuck it out for them to see. "It blinked right to Saturday noon. Now can you make it right again?" Juan was still worried about his watch.

"Sure. No problem." Jonas closed his eyes

again. From the gasp of the crowd, he knew he'd done it again. He opened his eyes, a big grin starting.

His smile froze as he looked over Sean's shoulder at the fence. On the other side the hatchet-faced stranger was staring straight at him. His yellow eyes reminded Jonas of a tiger.

The stranger's mouth was twisted in a horrible half laugh, half sneer.

AFTER SCHOOL Jonas went first to one door and then to the other. He went back to his locker, pretending he'd forgotten something. If he didn't hurry, he'd be the only kid left, and the guy sure couldn't miss him then. Jonas squatted beside his locker and peered inside, hearing his heart beat. The man's face was as bony and mean as a shark's. His eyes gleamed like a cat's after dark. Jonas's hands were cold and sweaty. He had trouble tying the strings on his backpack.

Suppose he threw the ball at the man? Tossed it as hard as he could down the street, then took off in the opposite direction? Wouldn't the man chase the ball, not him? But suppose it went down a storm sewer, got lost? The man would blame him. Wouldn't he keep coming day after day until he got Jonas?

Jonas McFee, A.T.P. Last night, lying in bed, he'd seen it all falling into place. First, take care of Sean Murdock. Jonas's rank in the fifth grade would be set. He could go on from there, doing wonderful things to amaze them all. Lisa Erickson, the cutest girl in class, would be writing notes to him instead of to Sean. He'd be walking home with her any afternoon he wanted. When he could fit it in. Jonas took hold of the metal locker and rattled it so hard he almost pulled the door off its hinges.

"Got a problem, hotshot?"

Sean Murdock was standing over him. Clearly, he was dying to know more about what Jonas had done at recess. Sean wasn't dumb, Jonas knew. A lot of show-off types were idiots. Sean was the opposite. He was smarter than most of the kids, and that kept him acting up all the time, in case somebody started to think he was a brain.

"What's it to you?" Jonas muttered, looking at the floor. All his dealings with Sean Murdock were in the past now. Jonas didn't need to be reminded about that one great moment when he'd seen it all coming true. Not now when he was facing death outside on the sidewalk.

Sean tried to seem cool. "Nothing. In fact, even less than nothing. Magic tricks are all fake. That's what you were doing—like that guy on TV that claims to read minds and saw people in half. Anybody's got to be a moron to believe any of that stuff."

"Yeah? You weren't really yawning, huh?

Gee—you want me to try it again? Maybe I can think up something—" Sean cut him off.

"Naw. Okay, so you did it. I didn't say you hadn't. But it's got to be a trick somehow. Some kind of thing you learned how to do."

Jonas was still kneeling in front of his locker. He stood up slowly and felt the bulge of the blue ball in his jeans pocket. Suddenly he was lonelier than he had ever been in his life. What could he lose now? It was all over anyway.

"Yeah," he said in a low voice, almost under his breath. "You're right, more or less. It's not me. It's something else."

"Yeah? Is it hard to learn, or what? Do you think you . . ." Sean swallowed, and he shifted his books to his other hand. "Look," he went on after a pause, "maybe we could trade something. Teach me about mind control, and I'll do something for you. You like Marvel comics? My uncle gave me his collection. Amazing stuff, back to the sixties. You could choose."

"Forget it," Jonas said in a dead voice. "It's all over." He reached into his pocket and snatched out the ball. He shoved it under Sean's nose. "See this? Well, this is all there is to it. This tiny ball. And it's not even mine. There's a guy outside just waiting for me to show my face. Then it's all over. He's going to kill me. I *heard him say* he'd kill me if he found me. Well, today at recess

36

he spotted me. As soon as I go outside, it's over."
Jonas tasted tears at the back of his throat. He
might be sobbing if fear hadn't dried up all his
spit. His head felt stuffed with cotton.

"*No kidding?*" Sean reached for the ball. Jonas
pulled it back. Even now he wanted to keep the
blue ball more than he had ever wanted anything
in his life. He was Jonas McFee, A.T.P. He had
powers he'd only begun to explore. Powers that
everybody in the world would envy. Jonas's face
had a glazed look, like somebody running a high
fever. His fingers had closed around the ball as
soon as Sean had glimpsed it.

"*How DOES* it work? Is it electronic? Was it made in Japan? Who's this guy?" Sean's questions poured out as he kept his eyes on Jonas's closed fist. Jonas was hiding the ball. "Show it to me again," Sean said.

Jonas stuffed the ball back into his pocket, shaking his head. "It's nothing to see. It just looks like a glass ball. It's after you get to see what it can do. . . ." He might as well tell Sean the whole story. What did he have to lose? He leaned back against the lockers and told Sean the way it had all happened. When he came to the part about the car floating, Sean looked longingly at Jonas's pocket. Sean was dying for one shot at trying out the ball. If he wasn't coming to the worst part of it, about the man's spotting him, Jonas would have smiled.

"So that's it. I don't know what to do. I've got to go outside. I can't stay in here. And as soon as I do, it's over."

"Suppose I help you?" Sean's voice was careful. Jonas knew he was figuring out just how to put his offer. "If I help you get away from this creep, will you let me in on the ball? So we can both use it?"

"What could you do?"

"Disguise you. The guy only saw you once. I'll go to the lost and found box and get some stuff that'll make you look different. I'll walk along with you. He won't be expecting you to be with somebody. And if he saw that recess act you put on, he'd *never* think we'd be together. He'd have to think we hate each other."

"You'd do that?" Could he get away from the man outside and keep the blue ball? Just share it some with Sean? That burning feeling he'd had before came back. "It would stay *my* ball. I'd keep it at my place and all."

Sean nodded. "I just want a chance to use it. I'm not asking you to give it to me. Deal?"

"Deal!" Jason felt a wave of relief so strong his knees let go for a second. "Where's the lost and found?"

"Wait here. It's in the office. I lose stuff all the time. They don't even bother to look anymore when I come in. I'll be back in a couple of minutes."

At the outside door, the two boys hesitated.

39

Jonas felt like a fool. Sean had brought him a lavender girl's parka with fake bunny fur around the hood and persuaded him to put on a pair of red-rimmed glasses he'd found in the box. They were nowhere near Jonas's prescription; he couldn't see at all. Sean, right next to him, was a moving blob.

"Do you see the man?" Jonas whispered, pulling the hood closer around his face, trying not to breathe the plumes of white fur. He knew by the way Sean was so quiet, the way he sucked his breath in before he answered, that, for sure, he had seen the man in the green coat.

"That is one nasty-looking guy," Sean said finally.

"Maybe we should try to hide inside," Jonas said desperately. "Until it's dark. Even all night." He had to go to the bathroom.

"Naw. It's okay. He's at the corner, checking both ways. He must have seen us, and he's not moved an inch. We're going to be home free. Just follow along beside me. We'll turn left at the main sidewalk, and he'll keep waiting there off to the right. As soon as I see a chance, I'll get us across the street. Once we get out of his sight, we can double back to get home. Where do you live?"

Jonas told him, and they started down the steps. He could look out from under the glasses and kind of see his feet in a fuzzy way. It was a nightmare, walking slowly, knowing the man's eyes were boring into him, not being able to see anything but wavy shapes. Jonas felt like a fish bumping along underwater.

"Where are we?" he hissed at Sean a minute or two after they'd cleared the steps.

"Shhh," he said. "We're doing great. Halfway to the street. Take it easy. Talk natural. If he sees us whispering, he might get suspicious."

Jonas didn't talk at all. He just trudged along, *slllooow* step by *slllooow* step, feeling as if he'd fallen into one of those stop-motion commercials on TV or a slow-motion instant replay. Sean nudged him to step off the curb and guided him across the street. With cars whizzing between them and the man on the corner, Jonas began to breathe almost normally. When they turned the corner and he knew they were hidden by the vacuum cleaner store, he felt so light he thought he'd float.

ONCE THE MAN couldn't see them, Jonas
put on his own glasses and shoved the hood off
his face. Then they took off like scared rabbits.
Jonas could feel those cat eyes boring into his
back, just between his shoulder blades, as they
ran all the way home.

"Here." He motioned toward the porch steps,
and Sean slowed. They both grabbed the hand-
rail and pulled themselves up. Jonas had a pain
in his side, but his relief was so strong he only
half noticed it. "I live upstairs," he was panting
to Sean, fishing in his pocket past the blue ball
for his key, when somebody came toward them
across the porch from the shadowy doorway to
the downstairs apartment.

"That is your door? I did not know. Excuse
me." The girl who had passed the ball through
the fence was suddenly there in front of him, on
his porch, just at the moment when he thought
he'd made it. Jonas sort of squeaked. Sean knew

who she was, of course. One look at Jonas would
have told him.

"I come to help," she said, standing in front of
them, looking small and miserable.

"My father . . ." Her voice dipped as if she
had choked on a sob. "My father is trying to find
you. He was waiting . . . I was very afraid."

"We're okay," Jonas said. He wanted to say,
And you can go away, but he didn't. Any minute,
she was going to be holding her hand out, thinking he'd just drop the blue ball into it. His body
tensed. It was his now. He'd fight to defend it.

"I am so glad," she said. "Seeing you makes
my heart sing. I was sick if my father—"

"Does he know where Jonas lives?" Sean's
voice cut in. "Does he know where you are
now?"

She shook her head. "He does not." But she
looked uneasily up and down the street. "If we
could go inside? You must hide. He must not see
me with you."

Jonas unlocked the door, and the three of them
went up the stairs.

"How come we have to be afraid of him if we
have the ball?" Sean said, halfway up. "I was
thinking, running over here—this is dumb. Why
not just zap the old goat? Give him a taste of his
own medicine?"

They were in Jonas's living room. The girl

didn't wait to be asked. She staggered across the room and sank onto the ratty old sofa. "Very comfortable, I am sure," she said, with a timid smile at Jonas. "I thank you." She looked white and very, very tired. Jonas remembered the panic on her face that first day. She must spend all her time running, hiding, trembling. "Do not try it," she said in answer to Sean. "You must never try it."

"Well, I can see if he is your father . . ."

"That is not the reason," she said. "He was my father. Once he was a fine, fine man. Genius. But who listened? They have small minds, those professors. . . ." Her golden eyes flashed fire. "He should have had the honor of the world. But they sneer at him. No one hears him. And so now he will make those who laughed sorry for it. He is so angry, he will destroy them all. He hates everybody. He will rule the world with this evil thing. He even taught it to tell him so. Radios, TVs—the ball can make them say he is the Powerful One. The Awful Terrible Powerful One, because he holds the ball. He loves to hear it. And he loves to make these plans. But we must stop him." Her eyes filled with tears. "In this, I must fight my own father. But do not think to use the ball against him. He *made* the ball. He alone understands its power. He alone is safe from it. He has made a shield. . . ." She put her face in

44

her hands. Clearly, she was exhausted.

"Would you like a drink?" Jonas felt silly, after what she had been saying, but he thought he ought to offer her something. "Some potato chips?" Through all this, he was waiting for her to come to the reason she was there—to get back the ball. "Finders, keepers," he muttered to himself.

Maybe it had been her ball once, but she'd stolen it from her father, hadn't she? And he had been planning to do terrible things with it. If a good person had it, someone like Jonas, think of all the wonderful things he could do.

Get his mom to quit smoking. Stop wars. Freeze teachers in their tracks when they started to pile on the homework. Nobody could ever ask him again to list the important products of New Zealand, he told himself, reaching into the fridge for three bottles of pop and shaking the rest of the potato chips into a plastic bowl so they could all reach them. He fought off feeling sorry for her. She was too feeble to keep the ball away from her father anyway. He and Sean were the logical people to use it now.

Jonas passed the potato chips to the girl and Sean. Each of them took a long swallow of cold sweet soda pop. Nobody spoke. Jonas was planning his words, getting ready to tell her he wasn't going to give back the ball, not yet. Not until he was sure it wouldn't fall into the wrong hands. That sounded right. He was pleased and opened his mouth to speak.

The girl sat upright and blurted out something she had been holding back ever since she had come in. "I am so sorry, but you must keep the ball for now. I cannot take it back. I am too weak, and he will find me. I hate to give you this burden. Many thousands of apologies for this hard thing I ask of you."

11

"*IF YOU* think that is the best thing," Jonas said carefully, not looking at Sean. "Today is Friday. And Monday is a teachers' day. We don't have school. So he won't know where to look." A moment of panic hit him. "How did you find my house? Won't he find out, too?"

She shook her head. "No. I learn your name. He has not. That is why I run. That is why I hide. He will do anything to learn your name."

"Gee," Sean said, "do you have a place to stay? Food and all?"

She looked embarrassed. "I am all right. In your country there are many sleeping outside. I lie on the sidewalk where the steam puffs out, to be warm. An old woman tells me where they give you food."

"That's awful," Jonas said. "You'll catch pneumonia." He tried to imagine being on his own on the street. He'd seen a girl curled on a piece of cardboard sleeping in the cavelike space under a stairway. He hated to think of *her* doing that, especially to protect him.

She looked puzzled. "But so many . . . how can your country think it is awful?"

"I don't know," Sean said. "I don't know why somebody doesn't do something about it. Do you, Jonas?"

"Maybe somehow with the ball," Jonas said in a dreamy voice. "Maybe we could point it at rich people and make them hand out some of their money. Maybe they'd bring out big platters of hamburgers, piles of grilled steaks, and let everybody dig in."

The girl looked frightened. "No. Do not think to use the ball now. You cannot."

"What do you want us to do, then?" Sean had been mostly listening. Now he put down his pop and hugged his bony knees, resting his heels on the couch. His eyes were big and serious. He looked like a grasshopper, perched at the other end of the couch.

"We came here, my father and I," the girl said, "to find a man. A professor who was his teacher many years ago at the university in our country. Professor Lapisthuler believed in him long ago. After the professor left, everybody laughed at my father, tossed away the papers he wrote. So my father came to find Professor Lapisthuler to see if he would join him. My father plans to destroy his

48

enemies and to make himself the ruler of all."

"Of *all?*" Sean laughed. "He doesn't think he can take over the United States?"

The girl looked down at her feet and twisted her fingers. "He would begin with your country because it is most powerful. The others would have to follow."

"That's crazy." Sean was trying not to be rude. "I know this ball is good, but we have nuclear weapons. Hydrogen bombs. Missiles."

"The ball would stop all machines from talking. No rocket could be told to launch itself. All bombs would sit locked in their cradles."

"Naw!" Sean looked uneasily at Jonas. "That's impossible! He couldn't do that, could he?"

Jonas nodded slowly, a light dawning in his eyes. "The Ahhvul Toval Pohpar has unbelievable power. . . ." His voice trailed off. Between his thumb and forefinger, the ball hummed with secret forces. Holding it, he suspected he could do anything.

All the crummy people who had ever given him trouble, all the hup, hup, hup gym teachers—what about that social worker who had come snooping around the year he'd goofed off in school? The lady who'd told him, "I like *you*, Jonas, but I don't like what you are doing. You do see the *difference*, Jonas?" She'd be zapped first of all.

He'd make her say what she really thought for once. "Jonas McFee, you are nothing but a crummy poor kid from a *bad home environment.*" Then he'd zap her right to the ground, clutching her fat middle, all her gold chains clinking together on the grass.

"So, do you think that will be a possible task for you boys, Jonas, my friend?" Jonas blinked at the girl's question. He'd been far away.

"Huh?" He looked dazed. Sean filled him in, giving Jonas a puzzled look.

"She said we should try to find this Lapisthuler guy. Tell him what's going on and get his help. She thinks maybe if he talked to her father, he could get him to be nice again. Give up killing people, turning everybody into slaves."

"My father is kind man," the girl said firmly. "When he sees his old teacher, I think he may come to himself again. This ball cannot have made my father a monster." She sat up straight, almost smiling. Her face was smooth as cream, with faint purple shadows under her eyes. Her blue-black hair hung past her shoulders, thick as a velvet curtain.

"We could go tomorrow and try to find him. Okay, Jonas?"

"Sure." Jonas squirmed. He liked the girl. He felt sorry for her. He had to do what she asked, as long as he didn't have to hand back the ball. "Sure, we can do that."

"Forever I am grateful. To have friends with whom to drink delicious Coke and to have such help, it is wonderful. In my country we do not tell both our names so early as here. Telling our names means we trust our friends. I am called Klarinda Fiar. My father is Jacobious Fiar."

She has a fairy-tale princess look, Jonas thought, that makes *Klarinda* right.

THE BOYS had a scrap of paper with two names written on it—Professor Hamish Lapisthuler and Jacobious Fiar. They took the university bus early Saturday morning, hoping to find the professor's office.

"I hope the place isn't all closed up for the weekend," Jonas said once they'd settled onto the bus. He had the ball in his jacket pocket. He was wearing his old coat since the good one was still at school. It was two sizes too small, and he kept checking to be sure the pocket wasn't holey. He had pulled a cap down over his eyebrows to the top of his glasses. Now he turned up his collar. He felt meaner that way, and better hidden.

Klarinda had told them her father would stick around the school, checking the neighborhood for Jonas. He would not look for Lapisthuler until he had the ball back. So, rumbling off on a smelly bus was a lot safer than hanging around home, Jonas told himself.

"Klarinda ought to come over here herself," Sean said crossly, "instead of sticking us with it." He pulled at the collar of his jacket and pulled his head in like a turtle.

"She has to stay close, to watch my house. To make sure he doesn't find it." Jonas sighed. Klarinda was as delicate as a baby deer. He was starting to like her more and more. He gently touched the ball, making sure it was safe.

"Well, if she wants to make sure we're okay, why doesn't she come *with* us?" Jonas didn't bother to answer. They both knew that if she were with them, the chances of her father's spotting them would soar. Complaining got their minds off being scared.

Yesterday after Klarinda had left and before Jonas's mom had come home—she was usually late on Fridays because she stopped for a beer after work with some friends to celebrate payday—Jonas had shown Sean how to use the ball. They'd done amazing things. With Sean on it, Jonas had made the sofa float up until it bumped the ceiling. Then he had it circle the room up there. Sean had tried to look as if he were having fun, but clearly he was scared.

They'd each tried flying around the apartment, from room to room, just high enough to fit under the tops of the doorways. Flying like that took concentration. Jonas had whammed his head into the kitchen wall when he'd let his mind wander for a second. Then they'd focused the ball on a dog who'd lifted his leg at the fire hydrant across the street.

He was a fluffy snowball of a dog, the kind that yapped and snapped on the end of its leash. Jonas made him stand there, like a statue, leg up. The lady with him stared; they saw her calling his name and tugging on the leash. The dog just stood there, leg up, frozen.

Once they'd let him go, Jonas and Sean rolled around on the floor laughing until tears rolled down their cheeks. Partly they were laughing because the lady looked so amazed. Partly they were laughing because seeing the dog made them think what they could do to people. The thought made them uneasy. They glanced at each other, and both thought things they didn't want to say out loud. Instead they acted like everything was funny and rolled around roaring.

But when Jonas had the ball, he knew he could make Sean collapse on the floor if he wanted to. He could make him feel terrible pain. Speed up his heart. Or stop it. He didn't want to, of course. But he *could* do it. Anything he wanted Sean to do, he could make him do. When he passed the ball over to Sean for a turn, he couldn't look right at him. He couldn't stand to see in his face that Sean was thinking those same awful thoughts about him. They did some wonderful things with the ball, but in a way they were relieved when they heard Jonas's mother unlocking the door. They rolled the ball to the end of Jonas's closet and pretended they'd been reading comics.

The bus rattled across town. The boys were quiet, uneasy with their thoughts. Finally they came to a block where enormous stone buildings lined both sides of the street. Sean pointed out the carving over the archway—Maximus University. Jonas pushed the buzzer, and they climbed off, along with a lot of college kids.

"Gee, look at this place," Jonas said. "I didn't know it was so huge."

"My mom's boyfriend brought me over here once," Sean said. "It didn't seem so big then. How can we even start to find Lapisthuler?"

"I kind of thought it would be like school," Jonas said. "One building with a sign up telling where everybody's room is." Instead, as he saw now, the university was a whole town unto itself.

13

THEY STOOD on the sidewalk and watched the bus pull away. "We've got to find a phone book," Jonas said. "That's what we should have done in the first place. We ought to call the professor up, tell him we have a message from Jacobious Fiar. Get him to meet us."

"That's true." Sean made a face. "We were dumb. It's hard to think when you're scared like this. Or kind of nervous," he corrected himself.

"Yeah!" Jonas was grateful for Sean's slip, grateful to have him beside him. Suppose he'd still been in this alone? He didn't want to think about it. Sean and Klarinda were both first-rate people.

They started down the street, looking for a store with a phone. On an ordinary Saturday morning Jonas and Sean could have had a blast over here. The university neighborhood had great stores. Terrific comics and places with all kinds of computer games. A shop midway down the block caught Jonas's eye.

COSMIC CRYSTALS, the sign read. The window was full of geodes and clear quartz crystals. Little cards in between the stones said, CREATE YOUR OWN REALITY and EMPOWER YOURSELF. CLEAR QUARTZ CRYSTAL IS A CHANNEL OF UNIVERSAL ENERGY, a long white card in the center said. POWERFUL TRANSMITTERS AND AMPLIFIERS OF NATURAL FORCES, another said.

"Look at this!" Jonas exclaimed. "Sean, other people must be on to this kind of thing, too. Maybe not as advanced as Fiar, but it has to be the same kind of thing!"

His granddad always said that the way not to be afraid of something was to learn about it. He'd told Jonas that, after Jonas nearly fried himself fooling with an electric socket. "With knowledge comes respect," his granddad told him. He'd drawn diagrams with + and − signs to show Jonas what was going on. He longed for somebody like his granddad now. This shop, with all its cards telling how stones might have mysterious powers, looked like the perfect place to learn.

"This looks great," Sean agreed. "Maybe we could even show them a little of what the blue ball can do."

Chimes hanging just inside the door made soft *wuoof, wuoof, wuoof* sounds as they went in. There was a long glass case with clear crystals in different sizes and lots of shelves of paperback books. A small crowd was milling around an archway in the back. BABU SPEAKS, announced a tastefully lettered blue sign beside the arch. Jonas and Sean started to join the line on the way in until Jonas noticed the rest of the sign.

$40.

He pulled on Sean's sleeve and got him out of line. They stood behind a bookcase and watched the people handing the man at the door two twenty-dollar bills apiece.

"Wow," breathed Jonas. "Can you imagine— all that money just to hear this Babu guy?"

The tall bookshelves hid them from the woman behind the counter. The man at the door was too busy checking the bills people handed him to look their way. They waited quietly for everybody to go inside, hoping they could hear what was going on.

Everything was very quiet. There was just a little creaking and coughing as people settled into folding chairs. Then, a long silence that made Jonas think that the Babu person must not have showed up. A voice started to speak in a deep, out-of-breath way. A woman. Indians on old TV Westerns talked the way she did.

"I Babu," the voice began. "Babu greets you beloved multitudes. How be you?"

Jonas heard gasps from the audience. "Time is a wind," the voice went on, pausing after every couple of words to let them sink in. "Forty-five thousand years ago, Babu stood in that wind. Today he blows to you again. There is only you. There is only me. Love the god that we are."

Sean frowned at Jonas. Neither of them could make out what the lady was talking about. Maybe if she got a little further along . . .

"Be you children today. Be you new children of the sun and of the wind. Ask you counsel of us, beloved children?"

Jonas took a step forward eagerly. The lady was going to answer questions. She must be some kind of fortune-teller. That's why people were laying out so much cash—to have her tell about the future. Boy, wouldn't he love to be in there? What's going to happen to the man in the green coat? Give me the future for Mr. Jacobious Fiar. Having *that* answered would be worth every cent of forty dollars. Sean was holding his hand against his upper lip, squeezing his eyes shut, trying not to sneeze.

"*Ptttccchhhuuuuuuu!*"

Sometimes holding a sneeze in makes it just

that much louder. That's the way it was this time. Sean looked embarrassed and wiped his nose with his scarf.

"Be you free as children. Honest liars. Birth yourselves today. Be born as children of the wind."

"Kids aren't allowed back here," the counter lady hissed at them from the end of the bookcase. She'd heard Sean and come to find them. "Babu's sessions aren't for children."

14

SHE HUSTLED them toward the front door. "We came to look at crystals," Jonas said, insulted by her nasty attitude.

"We have one of our own," Sean said. "A really rare one."

"We don't buy except from dealers," the woman said. "Recognized dealers."

Clearly, she didn't believe a thing they said. That, on top of the way the Babu person was ranting on about children while the store threw them out, made Jonas furious. He was beginning to wonder if the people in the store really knew all that much about crystals or about cosmic powers. He was beginning to think they might be a bunch of fakes.

"It's not for sale," he snapped. "It's way too amazing to sell." He pulled the blue ball out of his pocket and held it in his hand for her to see.

"That is kind of rare," the lady admitted, sounding surprised. "That's from a little country in the Himalayan Mountains, Himaltrya. Tiny little place. Only known source. I special ordered some yesterday for a foreign gentleman. Normally we don't carry them. They are more for decoration," she explained in a patient tone, like she was talking to idiots. "Our customers want quartz crystals. They learn how to clear them, and then they are funnels for cosmic forces. It's all a little over you boys' heads."

Sean snatched the ball out of Jonas's hand. Jonas was too frozen by what the lady had said to notice.

"Foreign gentleman?" Jonas took a deep breath. "Was he wearing a green coat? Did he have black hair, kind of amber-colored eyes?"

"Yes. That's him. Did you boys get yours from him? I'll tell him you stopped by when he comes in Monday afternoon. He had a rush put on them. Wanted all our supplier had. I *thought* he must be a dealer."

Jonas's mouth was dry. He turned to Sean, but Sean hadn't been paying attention to what he and the lady had said. He was standing there with the ball in the power position, aiming it toward the woman, a funny look on his face.

"No, Sean. Cut it out. Let's just go."

But the words were barely out of Jonas's mouth when Sean had the counter lady floating five feet off the floor, hanging in the air with her eyes big as an owl's and her face white as a sheet. For a second she hung there, still. Then she started to kick and squawk, flapping her elbows like wings, as if they were what was keeping her up.

"This crystal is just for decoration, and you look real pretty up there," Sean said. "I bet your puny quartz stuff couldn't do this, could it? Now what's over our heads? Tell me that."

"Cut it out! Let's get out of here!" Jonas grabbed Sean's arm, jostling him. The lady bounced crazily up and down. Her feet slammed against the cash register and rang up a sale.

"Serves her right," Sean snapped. "Trying to throw us out. Her crystals are nothing compared to ours. *Nothing.*" He raised the lady up two feet higher and swished her over their heads to bang into the wind chimes—*poof, poof, boing, boing.* He ran her back and forth through them, like somebody running his fingers down a piano keyboard. *Boing, boing, pong. Pong, pong, boing.*

"What the . . .?" The man who'd collected the money for Babu had come out of the back room to check on the noise. He stared openmouthed. Some of the audience trailed after him.

"The wind," one of them gasped. "The cosmic wind of Babu!"

"It materializes." A woman began to chant, "The cosmic wind of Babu. Time is a wind. Time cradles us."

Most of the audience had crowded out to stare at the counter lady hanging in the air. Then, wearing yellow silk pajamas, the Babu lady came out, too.

"What's going on?" she said in a normal voice.

"They've got some kind of magic crystal," a man blustered, turning red. "It's unbelievable. Help! Help!" The crowd was frozen, fascinated.

Sean just stood there with a glazed look on his face, holding the ball in the power position, looking directly at the counter lady. Jonas saw he was scared to death at the big scene he had going.

"Let her down," Jonas whispered in Sean's ear. "Easy. Go slow." He reached over and guided Sean. The control was partly in the way you moved your eyes and fingers, or you could guide it with your mind only. But that was tricky, and they were new at it. When the lady was a foot off the floor, Jonas took the ball back and pocketed it.

He grabbed Sean's elbow, and they ran for the door. The counter lady landed sputtering and lunged at them, but they were at the door and out. They ran down the street and turned the corner. No way would they look back. In the Cosmic Crystal people were too stunned to come after them.

THE DRUGSTORE they'd ducked into was dark and sweet smelling, like a cave with wooden booths and dim light. There was a gray and chrome counter with twirly stools lined up in front of it. An old guy wearing a white coat was behind the counter, drying a glass with a white dish towel. Jonas sank into a booth across from Sean, catching his breath. He waited for the man to say something nasty, like the woman in the crystal place. Maybe kids just weren't welcome over here, near the university.

"You gentlemen look a little winded," the man said, holding the glass up to check for spots before he replaced it on the shelf behind him. "Can I get you something?" He smiled across at them in a friendly way. He had white hair and a pink face that was kind of crumpled, like a pillow somebody had sewn a nose and droopy cheeks into.

Sean looked at Jonas, relieved. There was

even a phone booth over behind the magazine racks. "Let's have a Coke or something," he said, "before we try to call this guy." He drummed his fingers on the table. That crystal store lady had asked for it, and one side of him was glad he'd swished her back and forth through the wind chimes. But another side felt bad. She'd looked scared out of her wits, pumping her elbows like a plucked chicken trying to fly.

Jonas had a couple of dollars with him. "We'd like two Cokes, small," he called over to the man. He didn't look at Sean. He was furious. Sean had snatched that blue ball from the palm of his hand without saying a word. Like he had a right to it or something. Jonas McFee was the A.T.P. There could never be two of them.

"Cherry or plain?" The man had his hand on one of the handles in the long line of them at his soda fountain. Jonas and Sean had never seen a setup like this, except on old TV programs about the fifties. Jonas walked over to look, trying to calm down.

"You have syrup separate?" He climbed up on a stool to watch.

"Sure," the man said. He pumped the handle and squirted two bursts of dark syrup over the ice in the glasses.

"Cherry," Sean said, coming over. Jonas wanted plain. They watched while the man finished up with bursts of sparkling soda water that he stirred into the ice and syrup with a tall spoon.

"This is the best Coke I've ever had," Jonas said, taking a long sip through a straw.

"You ought to try the cherry!" Sean exclaimed.

"Glad to introduce you boys to the real thing," the man said. He chinked a spoon against Jonas's glass. "It's what you drink it *out of*, too. You boys stay away from those plastic cups with the snap tops. Coated with chemicals. Twenty years from now, half the world is going to have cancer. You heard it from me." His eyes twinkled as if he'd just given them great news.

"It sure tastes good," Jonas said. He hated talk about cancer. Every time his mom lit up, Jonas felt like telling her it might be starting, just a tiny white bud beginning to unfold in her lung.

Suppose he pointed the ball at somebody with cancer. Could he make it go away? Was *growing* tied to an electrical process in the body, the way thinking was? He just bet that it was. Give him a month or two and the chance to ask a doctor a few questions, and he just bet he could make cancer disappear.

Didn't they give a big prize for doing something like that? Off in another country? The Nobel Prize—and they had it for different things. Science, medicine, peace. Jonas took a deep pull on his straw, savoring the syrup at the bottom of the glass.

He could win *all* of them. Science would be a snap with the ball. Medicine he'd taken care of. Peace? Nobody would be able to get a bomb loose to drop it. He'd be on every talk show in the world. And money. Nobel prizes were worth lots. But never mind that. Money would be the last thing he was hurting for when the world found out he was the Ahhvul Toval Pohpar.

"Do you have change, Jonas? For the phone?" Sean broke into his thoughts. "Does your phone work okay?" he asked the man.

"Had it taken out fifteen years ago. When they wanted to put in one of those button things. I like a real honest twirler myself. Something flimsy about those new ones."

Jonas sighed. "We need to call someone."

"Use my personal one, here behind the counter. Long as it's local." He pulled up an old black phone like the one Jonas's granddad had. "You need the book?"

Sean nodded. "You have that piece of paper, Jonas? How do you spell *Lapisthuler?*"

The man looked interested. "That wouldn't be Hamish Lapisthuler? Professor of astrophysics, retired?"

"Is he retired?" Jonas looked sick. "We need to find him. It's an emergency."

"I didn't say he went anywhere," the man said. "In fact, if it's Professor Hamish Lapisthuler, retired, you want, you couldn't have come to a better place. Forget the phone."

"Why?" Sean wished the man would just spit it out.

"In half an hour, he'll be coming through that door. Sits in that booth over there. Has a Chicago red hot and hot fudge sundae. That's been his Saturday lunch for over fifteen years. Don't expect today to be any different."

I F THE COKES had been good, the Chicago hot dogs with mustard, chopped onions, and two kinds of relish were awesome. The hot fudge sundaes were made with the creamiest vanilla Sean or Jonas had ever tasted. Jonas had to shut his eyes while he ate the first spoonful, to take in the full effect. The fudge sauce turned chewy when it cooled off between the ice cream and the whipped cream. Salted pecans were sprinkled over it all.

As soon as they'd told Professor Lapisthuler they had a message from Jacobious Fiar's daughter, he couldn't do enough for them. He said they must join him for lunch. But Robertson's Drug Emporium was filling up with noisy college kids. It was hard to talk.

"After lunch we'll have more privacy, and you can explain what you want to tell me," he'd said, ushering them into his regular booth. Professor Lapisthuler was a small man with curly silver hair that sprouted in clumps around the bald spot on top of his head. He even had long silver hair growing out of his earlobes, Jonas noticed during lunch. His eyebrows ran wild. He looked like a yard somebody had tossed grass seed into. His eyes were the same muddy gold that Jacobious's and Klarinda's were.

He was wearing a stretched-out-of-shape sweater that bagged halfway to his knees and gray wool pants that he didn't seem to mind sloshing coffee on. But his face was sharp under all that gray hair. He wouldn't be easy to fool, Jonas decided, if you happened to want to try it.

Was he going to expect Jonas to hand over the blue ball? Was Klarinda? Well, he wouldn't. The professor was little, kind of light. A wimp, really. Jonas turned red. He was eating the hot fudge sundae the man had bought, thinking how he could flatten him. He leaned over his sundae glass, reaching with the long-handled spoon for the last hot fudge that had trickled into the narrow space at the bottom.

"Klarinda . . ." Professor Lapisthuler pulled a pipe out of his pocket, but he didn't fill it. He just ran his fingers over it. "Odd to think of a message from her. Just a baby when I left. A dozen years ago. How is she? Are they both here?" He stirred the fresh mug of coffee he'd asked Mr. Robertson to bring. The booths were clearing out. The drugstore was almost as quiet as it had been when Jonas and Sean stumbled in.

"She's fine," Jonas said, without thinking. "Well, no. She's not." He looked at Sean. It was hard to know where to start. "She's scared. She wants your help. Her father has invented something incredible. Almost unbelievable." Without thinking, he put his hand in his pocket and checked.

Professor Lapisthuler didn't look amazed or even especially surprised. "Does this amazing invention involve a blue crystal," he asked, "a blue crystal about the size of a large grape?"

"How did you know that?" Sean gasped. Jonas clutched the ball, hiding it in his fist.

"Jacobious had ideas, before I left, that were leading him that way," the professor said. "Some of his work was impressive, let me tell you that. I knew it would lead him into trouble because it would look crackpot to most of the scientific world, but he'd shown me enough to make me wonder."

"What about the blue crystal?" Jonas asked. "What did he tell you about that?"

Professor Lapisthuler tapped his spoon on the table. "Some crystals function well to tune and focus waves of various sorts. You boys may know that. Quartz crystals, for instance, are used to tune some kinds of radio signals. That property of crystals has led some people to think it might be possible to use them not only to focus waves, but to transmit them. I don't know if you noticed a shop on the way here, Cosmic Crystals?"

Sean turned red and looked down at his empty water glass. Jonas answered. "We noticed it," he said.

"Well, if you're thinking of going in there to see if they've picked up on Fiar's work somehow, save yourself the trouble." The professor rolled his eyes. "I stopped in when they opened. The woman behind the counter spouts a lot of mishmash." He paused. Jonas and Sean looked uncomfortable.

"This blue crystal is rare? Only found in Himaltrya?" Jonas was trying to change the subject.

"How did you . . .?" Sean started.

"Yes," the professor said, "they've been found in only one place—an unusual dent on the side of a mountain. Jacobious and I felt perhaps a meteor hit had caused it. He thought the crystals themselves were pieces of meteorite. Makes sense, because they do have properties unknown in any crystals we have found elsewhere on earth."

17

"WHAT WILL they do that other crystals don't?" Sean leaned his elbows on the table and folded a straw between his fingers. He and Jonas were curious. Just how much did Professor Lapisthuler already know?

"They have the ability to store and transmit energy. Jacobious convinced me of that years ago. It's the other part of his theory that you might find unbelievable. We all might."

"What's that?" They both spoke at once.

"His energy source. Jacobious Fiar wrote me he was about to tap into an entirely new source that would surpass any power we have thus far discovered on earth."

"Where would it come from?" Jonas was so caught up by what the professor was saying that he almost forgot they already knew the end of the story.

"A cosmic source—out in the universe. Space,

you boys might call it," the professor said. "But not exactly from *this* space."

"What other one is there?" Sean asked.

"You know about dimensions? What that means? Here. Think of a straight line pointing in this direction." He traced his finger toward them across the width of the table. "That's one dimension. Then think of the whole line moving sidewise in another direction." He ran his finger lengthwise down the table, out toward the soda fountain. "A flat area like this tabletop has length and width—two dimensions." He put his thumb and forefinger against the side of the table, measuring its thickness. "But look, here's another dimension. The up and down line that gives the table thickness. That's three dimensions. You boys follow me so far?" They both nodded.

"Okay. Here comes the hard part. Suppose we could find another direction we could move the whole tabletop through? Then we'd have a fourth dimension. The thing is, you can't picture that. *I* can't. Because all three of us live in three dimensions. But there is a fourth one. Actually, there are a lot more. There seem to be at least eleven dimensions, so far as we know."

"That's really weird!" Sean looked at the accordion crinkles he'd made in his straw and tried to picture twisting it through some direction that wasn't up, down, or sideways.

"Very," the professor said. "But, as it happens, the universe is exactly that. Weird. But now I'm getting to the part that bears on Jacobious Fiar's theory. Listen to this. When objects exist in space, the space itself is bent, warped. If the object is heavy enough, the space is warped so far that the dimensions sort of curl back on themselves. Suppose I dropped a bowling ball into a rubber sheet," he said, seeing their blank looks. "Imagine how the sheet would dip and stretch and cup around it."

Jonas frowned. He could just about picture it. His mom's bowling ball weighed a ton. Drop that on a rubber sheet, and the sag would pull the sheet together above it.

"What all this means," the professor went on, "is that a really heavy object can cut across from one dimension to another. That's what Fiar was counting on. He wrote me two years ago that he was sure there was an object—he called it a Y-star—that would come into our space about every three hundred years. Every three hundred years forty-five days, to be exact. It would remain for ninety-five days. He explained how he'd figured this out, but I won't go into that. The point is, this Y-star is orbiting another even larger star that's in one, or in *some*, of the other dimensions. We call something like that a transdimensional object. Because it crosses—the *trans* part—from one dimension to another. This Y-star puts out Y-rays, according to Fiar's theory."

"What are Y-rays like?" Sean was spellbound. He'd always wanted somebody to explain this kind of stuff.

The professor shook his head and sighed. "This was where I thought Jacobious might be coming unstuck. He claimed incredible powers for these Y-rays. He planned to store that power by using the rays to charge one of the blue crystals I told you about."

"What sort of powers?" Jonas looked at Sean. "Did he say it would do things like this?" Jonas brought the ball out of his pocket and set it in the power position. He lifted the professor's spoon and put it through two back flips. He brought the spoon down gently, beside the cup. Jonas thought how good he was getting now at controlling the ball. He'd never slam his head into the wall again flying around the kitchen.

"Precisely," the professor said quietly. "I would say that's just the sort of thing the Y-force could do quite easily. It could overcome gravity and allow objects, even heavy objects, to fly. It could also overcome and redirect all electronic impulses. In short, it could override all forces known on earth. Is that what you boys have there? Jacobious's crystal?"

The professor spoke mildly. Jonas had half

expected him to spring for the crystal as soon as he'd seen its powers. At least, he had expected the professor's eyes to widen in amazement. Instead, the professor knitted his fuzzy eyebrows. Far from trying to grab the ball, Professor Lapisthuler almost shrank back from it.

"*How did* you boys come by Jacobious's crystal? Surely he didn't give it to you? He wrote me he was making only one."

"Klarinda asked me to keep it." Jonas put the crystal back in his pocket. "She's afraid he'll do terrible things with it."

"Yeah," Sean interrupted. "She says he used to be nice. He's the meanest-looking guy I ever saw."

The professor frowned. "You must be in danger, Jonas. I could keep the crystal locked up in the lab."

Jonas stiffened. Just because he was a kid, the professor figured he could snatch the blue ball away from him. "No, thank you. I told Klarinda I'd keep it." He glared at the professor across from him in the booth.

"Are you sure he doesn't know how to find you?" Professor Lapisthuler looked worried. Jonas had clapped his hand over his pocket. He put his hand back on the table, feeling a little sheepish.

"Klarinda is taking care of that," Sean said. "She's making sure he doesn't learn Jonas's name, or figure out how to find his house."

"We've got to do something before school starts again. On Tuesday," Jonas said. "He'll find me for sure there. And we need to protect Klarinda. He's after her all the time."

The professor nodded. "You say Jacobious has new crystals coming in Monday?"

"He put in a rush order. The lady said she called her supplier."

"They'll come up from New York overnight express." The professor took a pull on his empty pipe, his eyes distant. "I see now where we'll find him, then."

"At the crystal store?" Sean sounded sick.

"No, no. I'll meet him when he goes to charge the crystals. To collect the Y-rays. Much better to see him alone." The professor was muttering along to himself, but Jonas was all ears. Jacobious Fiar was not going to make more blue balls. There could be only one A.T.P.

"How will he do that?" Freckles that usually didn't show stood out across the bridge of Jonas's nose.

"Well, what do you boys think?" The teacher was coming out in Lapisthuler. "A man needs to focus rays from space as efficiently as possible. What would he use for that?"

Jonas was dying, but Sean loved a challenge. He rubbed his finger into the initials carved in the booth, while he thought.

"A telescope?"

The professor smiled. "Exactly. Y-rays are in the range of light rays. These are a peculiar form of light ray, charged from passing transdimensionally."

"Well, there are telescopes everywhere!" Jonas groaned. "There's one in my closet at home!" His granddad had given it to him for Christmas a couple of years ago. They'd looked at the craggy surface of the moon and they'd seen the little dots that were Jupiter's moons.

"Jacobious will want a big telescope. An astronomical one. There's only one around."

"Where is it?"

"On top of Grizzly Mountain. The university's observatory. Couldn't be better for Jacobious's purpose. He'll be alone up there for all of Monday night. He could charge ten crystals in that time. I'll check my files, but I recall now that he said the ninety-five-day period for the Y-star to be in this dimension ends in February. He's probably only got a few days. He'll be desperate."

"You're going up there after him?" Sean shivered. Alone on a dark mountaintop with Jacobious Fiar.

"I'm going with you," Jonas said firmly. "And don't tell me how dangerous it'll be." He banged his fist on the table, angry even before the professor had a chance to speak. How else could he be sure Jacobious Fiar never made another blue ball? How else could he know there was one Ahhvul Toval Pohpar?

"It will be dangerous," the professor said. "But it's up to you. I don't choose for other people. I assume Klarinda will want to be there. Jacobious is her father, after all. But I would consider what you might be letting yourself in for, if I were you boys."

There was a long pause. Jonas leaned back against the booth, sweating a little. "If Jonas is going, I will go, too." Sean spoke slowly. "I said I'd help. I'm not going to chicken out now."

JONAS AND SEAN scrunched in the back of
the professor's battered Chevrolet. The car
lurched and swayed around the hairpin turns up
the mountain. One look at the dents in the professor's fenders had told them he might not be
the most careful driver going. Half an hour in his
car had left no doubts. How fast or slow he went
depended on what he was talking about. The
more interested he was, the closer he came to
rear-ending the car in front.

The ride across town had left the boys speech-
less. Now, at least, there were no other cars to
crash into. The professor spun into the hairpin
turns, spraying gravel behind them. Any minute
they expected the car to fishtail and slip off the
cliff. Jonas held the ball in the power position,
ready to fly the car back to the road at the first
hint of danger.

Klarinda was up front, beside the professor.
She was like someone walking through a bad

dream. "Thank you. Thank you a thousand times," she had told the boys on Sunday when they reported what Professor Lapisthuler had said. "Now I know it will be all right. On Monday night, his old teacher will talk to him. He will be himself again. I know that." She sighed. "Perhaps you should not go," she added. "The professor and I—we will meet him."

Jonas had reached out to steady her. And he had told her they were coming along. Now he could almost wish he hadn't.

But Jacobious was the only person between Jonas and full powers as the Ahhvul Toval Pohpar. The professor and Klarinda hoped to reason with him. Clearly, their hopes were dim. What would happen if Jacobious Fiar would not give up? The professor was very quiet about his plans for the ball anyway. Was he thinking to grab it himself? To make himself king of the universe?

Jonas looked at the back of the man's head, wispy as a dandelion gone to seed, bobbing back and forth as he wrestled the steering wheel around sharply, tires screeching. Maybe everyone, even a harmless-looking old guy like that, would secretly like to order everybody else around. He drove that way.

Jonas rolled the window partway down. The air was cold and full of the smell of pine. He took

85

a deep gulp of it and closed the window again. The road was a narrow twisting track between tall trees, spiky and almost black against the sky. After the sun had set, it would be dark as pitch up here. No streetlights, no car headlights, no neon signs. Just black trees and the whistle of the wind.

He looked at Sean, who grinned, but in a sick way. Their moms had been quick to let them come, once they'd heard Lapisthuler was a professor who wanted to take them up to the observatory. They'd even agreed to let Jonas and Sean spend the night at the professor's place, once they'd met him. He promised to drop the boys off at school on Tuesday. Jonas's mom was blown away by anything that looked educational, and Sean's was just as bad.

Jonas scratched his neck and then rubbed an itch between his shoulder blades. All his squirming and feeling halfway mad at his mom for letting him come wasn't going to help. It was his idea. He had to say the professor was one of the few people he had met who really respected kids. Clearly, he had wanted Jonas and Sean to stay back, but he let them come.

The car ground and sputtered up the last steep grade. They pulled onto the top of the mountain. The observatory was a tall building with a dome, black against the sky, which had faded to pale yellow. The professor bumped across the crude parking lot and out of sight behind a shed on the far side. They figured Jacobious would have a rented car, but there was no sign of it yet. No one else was there. Budget cuts at the university left the observatory empty most of the winter.

"Computers!" the professor had shrieked on the drive across town, slamming on the brakes moments before ramming a BMW. "For the business school! That's where all the money goes. Turning out more crooks and thieves for Wall Street!"

No one else would be here tonight. Just four of them, and Jacobious Fiar. Jonas and Sean climbed out of the car. Up here, above the trees, nothing stopped the biting wind. The ground was mostly rock, big slabs of granite that had worked their way through the ground. The earth's bones. Jonas shuddered.

"Be careful," the professor warned. "Over that way it's dangerous." Jonas read a sign: BEWARE— DEEP HOLES. "Cracks in the rock," the professor explained. "Drop down into caves, some of them very deep. The university used to have a fence over there, but it fell down. Those penny-pinchers are waiting for somebody to fall in before they put up another one." He blew on his fingers and pulled a knit hat out of his pocket. "Bundle up. Remember, there's no heat. Can't be. Would damage reception."

They all pulled out hats, scarves, and mittens. Swaying a little, leaning into the wind, they followed the professor to a squeaky door in the side of the building.

JONAS STEPPED into the dark. Emptiness
echoed around him. Sounds circled up and up,
lost in the height of the dome. Their voices were
small, like bugs cheeping. The professor snapped
on the light. Wood beams crisscrossed in the dim
heights of the dome. A ladder led up to the telescope on a platform twenty feet off the floor. The
telescope had a fat barrel, then a thinner one
tilted slantwise to the opening in the domed roof.

"The platform turns," the professor explained,
"rotates with the dome to view different sections
of sky." He showed them a desk at the foot of the
steep steps. He pulled a lever on the control
panel. With a grinding noise, the platform and
the rude wooden dome above them began to
turn. He switched it off. "Jacobious's Y-star is in
the northwest quadrant. Not much studied this
time of year. I'd love to take a look." His voice
was sad. "If only we had time. By dawn, the Y-
star will be gone. If Jacobious had shared this

earlier . . ." He looked sheepish. "If *I*, even *I*, his friend, had believed him earlier." He sighed and squeezed Klarinda's shoulder.

"It is not too late, Professor," she said eagerly. "I know you will reach him."

"How do you look through it?" Sean climbed a few steps toward the telescope. He was dying to know how it worked.

"You don't, usually," the professor said, "except with a camera. It's a reflector—uses a mirror. Rays enter the barrel, are collected on the mirror surface, and bounce to the focal point on the side. That's where they come together, to a focus." Sean nodded. "Jacobious will want to tie his crystals there where the film goes."

"Well, how are we going to stop him?" Jonas was feeling worse and worse. The next few hours would be the most important in his whole life.

"Klarinda and I will do that," Professor Lapisthuler said. "He doesn't need to know you are with us. See that door?" He pointed toward the opposite end of the room. "That's a storage closet. I want you and Sean in there with the lights off. If something goes wrong— If Klarinda and I . . ." His voice trailed off. "If things don't work out with us, you hide and wait. There's a telephone on the wall beside the closet door. If he's working the telescope, he won't hear you call. Get the police. That is *all* I want you boys to

90

do. Stay hidden and call for help. Under no circumstances should you try to deal with Jacobious Fiar yourselves. Do you understand?" His eyebrows bristled.

"Yes," Sean said meekly. "You and Klarinda will wait out here?"

"Exactly. You boys are safe, no matter what, as long as he doesn't know you are here. And Jonas is holding the only crystal with Y-rays. Don't try it against Jacobious's shield," he told Jonas fiercely. "That will turn the rays back against you. So *don't try it.*" His eyes bored into Jonas. "Don't let him know you are here."

"Okay. I won't." Jonas looked over at the closet door, avoiding the professor's gaze. "When do you think he'll come?"

"Soon. The Y-star rises around ten. He'll have to set the telescope to fix the crystals."

"Suppose he *does* make more blue balls?" Sean looked longingly at Jonas's jeans pocket. "Don't you think that might be better than having only one? People could share them. They'd balance each other out. Like our bombs and the Russians'."

"No!" Jonas shouted.

He was interrupted by the professor. "Too many unknowns," he said. "If only we knew they would be used for good . . ."

"There's only supposed to be one." Jonas

91

heard the blood rushing into his head, his eardrums throbbing. "This ball was the original. Others wouldn't be as good; others wouldn't be right." He stumbled over his words. "There is only *meant to be* one." Let somebody try it, he was thinking. Just let them try making more.

The professor frowned and was about to speak when they all turned away to listen. Faintly, still in the distance, they heard a car grinding its gears and backfiring. Someone was on the way up the mountain.

Hearts beating fast, Sean and Jonas dashed the length of the room and hid in the closet. They left the door ajar so they could hear. Peering through the crack, they could see the ladder up to the telescope platform. Professor Lapisthuler and Klarinda waited at the foot of it.

21

"*JACOBIOUS!*" The professor's voice rang out of the silence just after the boys heard the door to the outside being opened. "We were waiting for you." They tried to peer through the crack in the door. Jonas caught a glimpse of Jacobious Fiar's face as he crossed the floor toward Klarinda and the professor. He looked happy, almost human. For the first time, Jonas believed Klarinda's story about her father being a nice person before. Before he became the Ahhvul Toval Pohpar.

What if they could make him be nice again? Suppose Klarinda and the professor talked him out of trying to kill his enemies—out of making everybody else his slave? Wouldn't everybody think then that Jonas was going to give back the blue ball? If it worked out that way, how could he *not* give it back?

He would fight, yes, he would. He had the only blue ball. He would stop Jacobious from making another. He'd destroy the telescope if he had to. Overheat the wiring and burn the building to the ground.

The murmur of voices from across the big barn of a room was impossible to follow. After the first greetings, they stopped speaking English. But their voices grew louder. Jacobious was shouting, Klarinda was pleading, the professor sounded like he was making a speech. Himaltryan words were long, and full of drawn-out sounds—*aaiiee*'s and *uuuooo*'s like the wind moaning outside. *K*'s cracked like sparks flying. Deep hoarse sounds like the clearing of a throat. On and on the argument went, the voices more and more on top of one another.

"It's not going to work," Sean whispered, squatting in the dark beside Jonas. "Maybe we ought to try to go for the phone now, while they're yelling at each other."

Jonas blew on his fingers. He didn't want to wear gloves. That would make working the ball too tricky. The phone was on the wall just outside the closet door. Should they get the police up here as soon as possible? The professor could say Jacobious was breaking into the observatory and have him carried away to jail.

Jonas and Sean pulled the door open the barest sliver more.

The professor and Klarinda were in front of the

ladder to the telescope, blocking Jacobious's path. He was gesturing for them to clear out of the way. His back was to the boys, but even so they could tell he was stiff with rage. He held one hand out at an odd angle. Then he turned half around, snarling what must have been a command, and they saw why. He had a gun pointed at the professor and Klarinda. Jacobious was ready to shoot his own daughter.

Jonas was terrified. Sean's throat went dry. Seeing somebody with a real gun, ready to use it, was different from all the TV shootings he'd watched. Suppose Jacobious wheeled and shot *them?* Sean saw himself lying on the floor with blood oozing out of his mouth, eyes staring like fish in the grocery store. "Jonas," he whispered, "listen, we've got to do something. Maybe we should try to get out of here."

Jonas froze. Any sudden move and the man might sense they were there. He remembered Sean's sneeze in the crystal shop and felt an itch rising in his nose. Frantic, he pressed his upper lip and sucked in a deep breath. The itch passed. Weak with relief, he turned to Sean. "We have to wait," he whispered. "If he gets up to the telescope, we'll move. He's not going to shoot Klarinda. How could he?"

Jonas kept telling himself that. Who could hurt his own daughter?

95

His question stopped midway. A loud crack rang out. Jacobious had fired the gun.

The professor had jumped in front of Klarinda and turned in rage to face Jacobious. He was a brave guy, wispy as he looked. Neither of them was hurt. Jacobious waved the gun, directing them away from the ladder and to the side. The professor's face was lit by the bare bulb hanging over the desk and control panel. Jonas saw a twitch that meant he was being careful *not* to look in their direction.

Jacobious Fiar ordered them off the ladder toward the wall opposite the closet. Craning his neck, Jonas saw where they were headed. A pile of rope was coiled beside the door. Jacobious planned to tie them up. Just when Klarinda and the professor reached the wall, Jonas saw the professor lunge suddenly backward with his elbow, toward the light switch. The whole observatory was plunged into darkness.

22

GRUNTS AND THUDS echoed in the blackness. They were struggling.

Sean thought of groping his way along the wall to the phone. But he knew he couldn't dial a number in the dark. And suppose Jacobious switched on the lights while he was standing by the phone? Out in the open? The only thing he could do was to hunch in the dark closet with Jonas, and pray that the body he heard crashing against the opposite wall was Jacobious's body.

The light came on—almost blinding after the total dark. The boys squinted to see. A body was crumpled on the floor. They recognized the professor's gray sweater, and their hearts sank. He wasn't moving.

Jacobious turned away from the light switch and held the gun on Klarinda. She was crying. Gruffly he ordered her against the wall. He quickly tied her up, twisting a long coil of rope around her and knotting it behind her back.

Then he straightened and nudged the professor's body with one toe. To their horror, Jonas and Sean saw that the professor didn't groan or stir. He just lay there.

Jacobious dropped the rope. Obviously he'd decided there was no need to tie the old man up. He headed for the telescope control panel. Jonas watched him at the controls, rotating the telescope to the northwest. He watched Jacobious flip the switch off and head for the ladder. Jacobious reached into his pocket on his way up. Cupped in his hand, blue crystals caught the light.

Jonas began to form a plan.

Careful to keep his fingers folded around the ball, not to let its light shine out even though they were safely hidden inside the closet, Jonas took the blue ball out of his pocket.

"What are you doing?" Sean hissed, frightened. "Don't get that out now. We've got to wait until he's busy up there with his back to us. Then we'll go for the phone. That's all it'll take. You can't try anything fancy." Sean's voice pleaded. He was scared Jonas would do something dumb and bring them face to fang with Jacobious Fiar. The man's eyes were like a mad dog's. His lips curled back, and Sean almost expected him to slather. Sean shuddered, remembering how

Jacobious had looked when he'd straightened up from tying Klarinda.

"I'm not going to let him get started with those crystals," Jonas whispered back. "If he charges more crystals with Y-rays, what good will all the police in the world do?"

"We just have to hope he won't have time. They've got to be there long enough to soak up energy. We just have to hope that'll be an hour or so. The professor said . . ."

Jonas cut in. "Yeah, and look where he is now."

Sean felt with a chill how much Jonas had changed. Just two days ago, he'd been making Juan's calendar digital watch jump forward, laughing and playing tricks. Two days ago he had wanted Sean's help, and he'd made Sean think he wanted them to be friends. Now Jonas wasn't listening to anybody. He was making the rules himself.

"All I'm saying is that it's dangerous. We ought not to take chances if there's another way." Sean snuck a glance sidewise at the crystal in Jonas's fist. If Jonas loosened his fingers just a touch, if Sean could get him looking away, maybe he could grab the blue ball away from Jonas. He remembered how he'd felt floating the woman up to the ceiling. That ball made you forget about being a human being. With that ball, you didn't need to be nice. You were a god.

"I won't let him even begin to make another blue ball," Jonas said. "That's final. If I have to take a chance or two, I will." He reached to pull the door open farther, clenching his jaw so tightly the muscles trembled in his cheek.

Sean couldn't wait. In a minute Jonas would be out in the open, getting them both killed. Jonas didn't deserve the ball. Sean knew he could handle it. He saw the blue fire through Jonas's clenched fingers. With a sudden lunge he pried Jonas's fingers apart and grabbed for the ball. It slipped away from them both and rolled out of the open door, glowing and shimmering with its strange circle of light. It stopped out on the floor of the observatory, ten feet from the closet door. In plain sight. All Jacobious Fiar had to do was to turn his head. His eyes would be dazzled by the sight.

JONAS DIDN'T care about Jacobious Fiar and his gun. He wanted the blue ball. He lunged out the door and dived full length, falling on the ball. After he grabbed it, he felt himself breathe again. He felt the power surge through him as his hand closed on its roundness. He wanted to kill Sean. Without the ball Jonas was nobody. That pulsing was like the beating of his own heart.

Jonas flipped the ball into the power position and scrambled to his feet, wheeling toward Sean. Sean was the real enemy now. Worse than Jacobious Fiar. Look at Sean's pale face. Scared to death! Make him squirm. Drop him to his knees. Jonas heard a faint, high-pitched whine as he directed the ball's force to jolt Sean off his feet. Zap! He slammed him backward against the wall like a mosquito. Splat!

"Help!" Sean cried. Then he hit the wall and crumpled, like the professor, to the floor. The air smelled burnt from the force crackling in Jonas's fingers. He loved the smell.

"So! You have my ball. We meet at last." Jacobious Fiar was leaning over the railing to the platform, grinning. "I think you will return that to me. I think you will drop that ball at once." His gun was pointed at Jonas's heart.

Jonas had gone past fear. He felt almost happy. He was dizzy with the chance to go against Jacobious Fiar. To win at last. That was why he had come. The ball was useless against Fiar. He knew that, but Jonas had figured out what to do. As soon as Fiar climbed up the ladder to the platform, Jonas had known he could get away from him.

Jonas pointed the crystal toward the control panel. At the same time, he stepped forward. "Okay," he said. "Okay. You win. Here, I'll give you the ball."

"NO!" Fiar snarled down at him. "Drop it! No tricks or you are dead."

But Jacobious wasn't fast enough.

The moment he'd stepped forward Jonas had powered the motor that rotated the platform on which Jacobious stood. Gears squealed as Jonas made the platform twirl faster than it was ever meant to spin. Jacobious Fiar and his gun blurred as they spun out of control.

The dome motor would burn out in a few minutes. Jonas dove for the outside door.

He could take the ball and fly off. Escape Fiar completely. But then the man would have the chance to power the other crystals. Jonas couldn't be sure he'd wrecked the telescope motor or that Fiar wouldn't have some other way to focus the Y-rays. It had to come to a contest between the two of them. Should the world have an evil Ahhvul Toval Pohpar or a good one like Jonas McFee?

Jonas raced across the parking lot to the field just past the space the professor had warned them about. He grabbed the sign and tossed it behind a bush. Fiar wasn't to know about the danger. Jonas hoped to trap him. If he slid into a cave, Jacobious Fiar would be trapped until somebody lowered a ladder to haul him out. And then he'd be in jail. In a few hours the Y-star would be gone. All Fiar's chances would be gone.

Jonas raised himself a foot off the ground and zigzagged across the boulder-strewn field watching for the perfect place to lie in wait for Jacobious. The ground was dotted by dark blobs, holes that dropped into the caves the professor had mentioned. What he wanted was a nice hole that didn't show until you were right on top of it. A nice drop that Jacobious Fiar wouldn't see before he sank down. A wide slit between two boulders looked just right. Jonas lowered himself to the flat surface of the rock just past it.

Gingerly, he leaned over the gaping hole. How deep was it? He pushed aside the thought. So Fiar broke a leg or something. Tough. Look what he'd done to the professor and his own daughter. Maybe he'd break his neck. Jonas's eyes gleamed, cold as the crystal in his hand. He grinned a grin as nasty as the one he'd seen on Jacobious Fiar's face a few minutes earlier.

Jonas knew how Jacobious Fiar thought. He understood him as well as he understood himself. Nothing but the crystal mattered to Jacobious. If he thought he could grab it, he'd leap straight into nowhere, without looking. But nobody would outsmart Jonas McFee. Not while he had the blue ball shining in his fist.

THE MAN was like a zombie, waving his arms and teetering on the tops of boulders. He stood on a tall rock in the starlight—there was no moon—and sniffed the wind. Jonas had always thought of Jacobious Fiar as a hound. A skinny yellow-eyed hound loping along after him, after him until there was no escape. Tonight Jonas wasn't planning to run.

"Over here!" Jonas's voice floated, sounding weak and sad on the cold wind. Jacobious's eyes lit up, and he turned in the direction of the call. "Help me!" Jonas cried. "I give up! You can have the ball. I can't get it. Help me!"

Fiar smirked and set out across the field. Jonas had chosen the path well. There were no holes gaping along the way to warn Fiar of danger.

"My foot! It's caught! My ankle! I think it's broken!" Jonas wailed in agony, and Jacobious Fiar grinned in triumph. His big feet thudded along the ground as he bounded toward the place where Jonas crouched. Lodged halfway up the boulder behind Jonas, the blue ball flickered with its eerie light. Jonas had stuck it in a small crack in the rock, where it might have fallen, if he had tripped trying to escape.

If Jacobious was going to reach for it, he'd have to stand just down there, at the foot of the big stone. Jonas looked at that darker darkness and smiled. But he was covered with cold sweat. Suppose it didn't work? Suppose Fiar looked down at his feet, not up at the crystal? He wouldn't. He couldn't. If the crystal was almost in his grasp, Fiar wouldn't look at anything else.

Fiar came clambering over the first rock. "So, you give up? I thought so. Worms. You are all worms." When Jacobious saw the ball, his face radiated pure delight. "Ah," he exclaimed, "it is here, then? My star, I will have you back." Fiar jumped lightly down to the space between the two rocks, already reaching for the crystal, rapture in his eyes. And disappeared with a long wail that echoed up from the depths at Jonas's feet.

Jonas tried not to hear him hit, but he did. A distant awful crunch. Jonas thought he felt the ground shudder. He held back the urge to wet his pants and shivered, feeling sick. He clenched his jaw trying to stop his stomach and throat from heaving. They'd never pull Jacobious Fiar out of there. Never carry him off to jail the way Jonas had planned. Jacobious Fiar was dead.

Jonas looked up at the crystal glowing above him and almost hated it. What had it made him do? He closed his eyes and tried to clear his head. He wasn't thinking straight. It was an accident. He wasn't awful like Fiar was. He stood up and crawled carefully up the rock to retrieve the crystal. His now. For sure. Forever.

Now he could cure cancer. Make anything he wanted to happen, happen. Would he use it for tricks first, just to get used to it? Be on talk shows and all? Then go for the serious stuff. Maybe hire a staff to research into what might be done. Scientists like the professor . . .

His thoughts broke off. The professor and Sean were lying inside, unconscious. Maybe dead. Sean. It was Sean's idea to get the disguise from the lost and found. Saved Jonas's bacon that day. Jonas swayed on his feet. He kept hearing Jacobious Fiar's last wail, crying up from the hole at his feet. For a second he even thought the voice he heard floating toward him out of the dark was his.

"Jonas! Father! Father! Do not hurt Jonas. Please. Spare him. My fault. Father, blame me!" Klarinda's tearful voice cut into Jonas. She'd managed to untie herself and stumble out to try to save him. He tried to call to her, but his throat closed. How could he tell her? He had killed her father. Just a minute ago, he had felt so certain of himself. Jonas McFee, A.T.P. Wasn't that everything he'd ever wanted? What else could there be?

"Klarinda!" he called. "I'm okay. Wait! Wait there. Remember the holes! The professor said . . ." He scrambled onto a rock and looked over at her, running onto the field from the parking lot. "Stop!" But he was too late.

With a gasp, Klarinda slipped and fell. Her white blouse had been a ghostly shape in the starlight. Now it was gone. Jonas stared at the empty space where she had stood. Forgetting to use the ball, he stumbled across the field toward the spot. A muffled call came up to him from the ground under his feet.

"Jonas . . . Jonas . . . help me! I hang here. Help me!" Jonas leaned over the edge of the hole. He smelled the damp cave air and heard a trickle of water far, far away.

"Where are you?" he called down to her.

"Who can say?" She was sobbing. "The dark will choke me! I will die!" Her voice sounded far away.

"Did you land on something? Is there a way back up?"

"A ledge. I feel a ledge. Oh! Then it falls."

Jonas heard a stone dropping, dropping away for

an impossible time. Then a tiny splash. An underground river, hundreds of feet down. If Klarinda slipped, she would fall all that distance to the water.

"I'll drop you a rope. Wait. I'll go get the rope. Can you hold on that long?"

"Yes. I wait. Bring the rope. Oh, thank you. I wait."

JONAS WAS back with the long coil of rope Jacobious had used to tie Klarinda. She'd dropped it just outside the door when hurrying to run after him. Jonas dangled it into the hole and lowered it hand over hand, swinging it back and forth. "Is it coming?" he called down. "Do you see it?"

"See? But the dark, Jonas. I cannot see. Where is your rope?"

"Here. I'll swing it from side to side." But Jonas was feeling more and more hopeless. The chance of making the rope brush up against her so she could grab it wasn't good. He needed something to loop it around, a tree trunk or something to pull her up. And if she did feel the rope, she might lunge for it and lose her balance. Damp rock was slippery. They had to have a light. Did the professor bring a flashlight?

Then he realized. Why was he messing with ropes and flashlights? The answer was in his pocket. He pulled out the glowing crystal. He held it in the palm of his hand, seeing its eerie mysterious beauty, its power glowing and pulsing. He leaned over the hole, hoping for a glimpse of Klarinda. To bring her up he had to see where to point the rays. He knew there had to be a way to make it work in the dark, but he hadn't had that much practice. He'd always seen where to point it. He peered down, down. Nothing but blackness. The circle of light from the ball petered away in the dark. He could hold the ball between his thumb and forefinger and float to her. Bring her up.

He held the ball in the power position and lifted himself up over the hole. A sickening lump rose in his throat. The dying wail, the distant thud of Jacobious were in his ears still. He was shaking. The ball almost slipped from his fingers. Jonas was covered with a chilling sweat. He couldn't do it. He couldn't go down there. He saw himself crushed at the bottom like Fiar. He brought himself back to the ground and slumped there.

"Jonas?" Klarinda's voice was weak. "You are there still? Am I right? With your rope?"

"Yeah. Yeah. Listen, Klarinda. Hold on. Stay perfectly still. I have a plan. You'll be okay. You'll be fine. Just wait a minute." He hauled the rope back up out of the hole. The end was frayed into lots of separate strands. Jonas wove them quickly into a nest for the blue ball, knotting it carefully in place. The end of the rope glowed bright blue as he lowered it into the dark. A two-foot circle of light. She couldn't miss it. "I'm sending the ball down, okay? Take it out of the rope, and use it to bring yourself up. Okay?"

For a long minute or two there was no reply. Then he heard her voice, warm with relief. "Oh, yes. I see. Stop. It is here. I have it now. I am saved." Jonas felt the rope moving with her attempt, down below, to untie the ball. He knew she was all right. He backed away from the hole and sank to the ground, too tired to move. He buried his face in his hands, somehow not quite wanting to see Klarinda coming up from underground holding his blue ball in her fingers. He had given it away.

He felt a hand on his shoulder. The professor knelt beside him, his face twitching. A lump on his foreheard was turning purple. "You are all right, Jonas? Where is Jacobious?"

Jonas began to answer, then stopped as Klarinda appeared, rising up at their feet. The crystal flashed blue fire in her hand. She settled onto the bumpy ground beside them. Jonas reached toward her.

"Give it back now." The cold blue fire swept

across their faces like the flickering lights that came sometimes in the northern sky. Jonas had stared up at them in his granddad's yard, awed by the crackling of cosmic electricity. Holding the ball made Jonas master of powers more distant and strange even than those. The Awful Terrible Powerful One. "It's mine now." He was ready to hurl himself against her. Shove her back down the hole. "You *gave* it to me."

Klarinda trembled, a deep shiver that ran all through her body. For a long minute she stared at the crystal in her fingers. Then she held it out over the hole in the earth and turned it loose.

"I am sorry, Father," she said. Jonas dove after it. The professor grabbed just in time to stop him from slipping. But Jonas saw it fall, the blue fire burning dimmer and dimmer and then, finally, a faraway splash.

None of them said anything. They all thought the same thoughts. If only . . . if only . . . think of all the good . . . think of all the possibilities.

Jonas felt hollow, empty, erased like a word on a chalkboard.

Finally the professor spoke. "Even Jacobious might someday understand," he told Klarinda.

Jonas hadn't told them. Like somebody talking about the past, about what happened weeks ago, he said, "I'm sorry, Klarinda, but he is dead.

Your father fell. He was after the ball, and he slipped." Did he have to tell her he set it up? Not now. Maybe later.

Klarinda nodded. "I knew. I thought. Now his ball is with him, yes?" She turned to the professor, catching hold of his jacket, and sobbed.

"Sean," Jonas said in a deadened voice. "I slammed Sean into the wall. I don't know if he's . . ."

The professor shook his head. "No. He's groggy, but all right. I told him to stay inside until he was steady on his feet. In a moment he should come looking for us." They looked over at the observatory building. A square of yellow light appeared as the door opened.

"Jonas? Are you okay?" Sean wobbled onto the steps. "Professor? Where are you?" He came toward them.

They went to meet him.

*J*ONAS WAS NOT the A.T.P. He ate beans
and spaghetti with his mom and watched their
fuzzy old TV set. He tried to get his mind on set-
tling into his room and putting his stuff away.

"Brought you something, kiddo," his mom
said Wednesday night, fishing into her purse.
"Batteries. For that robot Dad gave you. So it
won't sound like the *Mummy's Revenge* anymore, okay?"

"Great. Thanks, Mom," he'd mumbled.

At night Jonas lay in bed and remembered and
thought and prayed to have the ball back until
his ears hummed and his eyes were scratchy as
sand. He pictured the ball lighting up the river-
bed inside the mountain. Probably it had caught
against a stone. Probably the water eddied past
it, glowing blue. Fish in a place like that were
blind. They would nose up against it, feel it
pulse, and jump back from the shock.

He and Sean talked at recess and after school

about how they'd find a way to go after it. Lower themselves with ropes down the shaft. Get hats miners use, with lights on them. Wear rubber suits and wade the river. How hard could it be?

"We don't know how wide the shaft is, though," Sean had said. "It might get too narrow for a person."

"Dynamite it, then," Jonas said. "We could blow up the mountain if we had to. Sift through the pieces until we came to it. How important is a dumb mountain? How important is *Anything* when you think what that ball can do?" Then he looked away. He knew what Sean was thinking.

Sure, how important was *he?* Hadn't Jonas tried to smash him like a fly? Jonas kept remembering how he had done that. He tried not to, but it kept coming back, like it was some other person he had been. And he heard the long sad wail of Jacobious Fiar every night, just when he was about to sleep.

"I wanted the ball, too, you know," Sean said, sort of dragging the words out. "It wasn't just you. I thought of how I might get it for myself. How I might keep it. Really, I was grabbing it for myself that night. If you hadn't slammed me, I would have zapped you. That's the truth."

Jonas struggled with his thoughts. "We could work out something," he said. "A plan on how to share it. Then when we get the ball back, we can both use it." Maybe they could have a big office building—BLUE BALL ENTERPRISES. With different branches. Medical, scientific, one for stopping wars. By then Klarinda would be feeling better about the ball and come in with them. Jonas could be the CEO, and Sean and Klarinda could be the division chiefs. They'd keep the ball in a safe in Jonas's office. Would he tell the others the combination? Jonas figured there'd be plenty of time to iron out details later.

Professor Lapisthuler and Klarinda weren't as interested in talking about getting the ball back. Sean and Jonas met them for Saturday lunch at Robertson's drugstore. The professor was fixing up Klarinda's visa so she could stay with him. Going back to Himaltrya without her father or anybody who understood what had happened would be hard.

"Sean and I are going to look for the ball," Jonas told them. "When we grow up."

"Are you?" Professor Lapisthuler sighed. He mopped a spot of mustard off his sleeve "I am thinking of leaving notes. For when the Y-star returns. By then, perhaps people might be ready."

"That's not for THREE HUNDRED YEARS! We'll all be dead!" Jonas worked his straw up and down in his ice.

"Good." Klarinda had been quiet while they talked about the ball. Now her voice was cold. "I never want to see the evil thing again. It should live in the dark with the bats and the fishes."

"The usual for dessert?" Mr. Robertson smiled down at them in his white drugstore jacket. "I'm toasting pecans. They're coming up crisp and hot."

Jonas and Sean looked at each other. Years would pass before they'd be old enough to get into the mountain and find the ball again. There would be a lot of Saturdays at Robertson's drugstore before then. The thought made the long wait less painful, that was for sure.

Professor Lapisthuler held up his glass. "I want to propose a toast," he said. "To somebody who is a little bit of a hero, I think."

Jonas paused, stabbing his straw halfway down. Sean, maybe? He had come along with them just to help. And Jonas had nearly killed him. No, Klarinda, probably. She could have been a princess. Mink coats, diamonds, VCRs, and every computer game in the world. Instead, she'd tried to save everybody else. He lifted his glass, ready to drink to her.

"To Jonas," the professor said. "He chose to save a friend. We all know what he could have chosen instead." He smiled warmly, his glass raised to Jonas.

Jonas turned red. "I . . . I . . . I . . ." He remembered holding the ball, seeing it flash. He remembered what he had thought, how close he had come.

Klarinda smiled shyly at him from across the booth. "I thank you, Jonas. I thank you again."

For the first time, he felt a little proud.